The Horrors of Seward Shores

P.A Douglas

SEVERED PRESS
HOBART TASMANIA

The Horrors of Seward Shores

Copyright © 2016 P.A Douglas
Copyright © 2016 by Severed Press

WWW.SEVEREDPRESS.COM

ISBN: 978-1-925493-69-6

Author's Note

Although Seward, Alaska, is a real place, I have taken some geographical facts out of context to better suit the purposes of this piece of fiction. After all, that is what this is: fiction.

Author's Acknowledgments

For this first edition of *The Horrors of Seward Shores*, I wanted to thank everyone at Severed Press for all the hard work they do. And for supporting my desire to create and sell patches. I also wanted to thank *Dane Hatchell* for being an extra set of eyes on this book. That is always a big plus. And it really does make me seem like I know what I'm doing as a writer. So, thanks Dane. I also want to thank *Google* and *Wikipedia*. This was the first book I really had to do my homework for. So, for that…thank you, Internet.

Other Severed Press titles by P. A. DOUGLAS

The End with co-author Dane Hatchell
The Dark Times with co-author Dane Hatchell
Epidemic of the Undead
Rainbows and Sunshine…and Zombies
The Old One
Killer Koala Bears from Another Dimension
The Dark Man
Hitchers
Rancid
Watchers

Things people say about P. A. DOUGLAS

Prologue

"Come on, Kevin. What the heck we doin' out here anyhow?"

"I'm tellin' you this here's the spot." Kevin pulled the tiller in toward his chest. "Help me with that-there boom. Push it out to the left. We're goin'a drop anchor right here."

Rick rolled his eyes. It was early. It was cold. And he was tired. He wasn't even sure how Kevin had talked him into setting sail this early in the morning anyway. Sure, the first week of November wasn't the absolute coldest month in Alaska, but it wasn't warm. Sitting there, with leggings on, two pair of socks under his boots, and the thickest jacket he owned, Rick was freezing. It wouldn't be so bad once the sun was out, but that wouldn't be for another few hours. He tried to count his blessing. At least the wind wasn't kicking up too hard. No matter, his teeth still chattered and his butt was wet. But, all of that didn't matter. They were here now. Might as well make the best of it.

Rick and Kevin were best friends going all the way back to middle school. Heck, that was a lifetime ago. It is surprising how quickly thirty years can fly by, even with nothing better to do than visit the local pub and cast net for a living. Both men were in their early forties now.

Although Rick had never married, having lost his high school sweetheart to an accidental fire, Kevin, on the other hand, was three and 'O'. Constantly on the hunt for wife number four, the two men had a lot more free time to spend hanging out together now that Kevin wasn't married to that *Jezebel* of a wife number three, Mandy. Nothing to do but drink beer, cast nets, and watch sports at the pub.

But that's just how the Kenai Peninsula Borough of Seward, Alaska, was. Seward was a quiet fisherman's port style community. With a population of only fifteen hundred people, when you didn't count the tourists, it was no wonder that everyone knew *everyone*. That didn't mean everyone got along, by any means, but such was the way of small town community living. Most folks who lived here made their living as either commercial fishermen or as portside hands who dealt indirectly with the trade in one way or another.

Rick secretly thought that might be part of Kevin's marital problems. How can any man expect to keep his wife happy if he tends to be gone at sea for several months at a time? Even though Rick wasn't seeing anyone, that factor was one of the main reasons he preferred to simply work for the postal service. Good hours, great benefits, and home in time every night to feed the cat and catch up on old reruns of the X-Files and Judge Judy. But not Kevin. He lived on a boat. And he went out on long-term jobs as often as he had the opportunity to. So, when Kevin wasn't out on a job, it was a treat for Rick that they spent a little time together as old friends. Even if it meant waking up at the butt-crack of dawn to be on the cold, salty water in a rickety sailboat in November.

That's actually what Rick was thinking about when Kevin's voice chimed in again, this time with a shove to the shoulder.

"Hey, man… you hear me?"

"Sorry, Kevin." Rick shivered, rubbing his shoulder with a gloved hand. "Got lost in thought there for a second, I guess."

"*You guess*, is right." Kevin lifted the anchor, about to drop it into the water beside the boat. "You look like one of them-there zombies on the Walking Dead show."

Rick smiled.

"Kick that boom out for me. We need the mainsail out of the way so we got room to cast the net."

A sudden, loud splash pierced the silence around them as Kevin let go of the anchor. The rope tied to it whizzed as it rubbed across the side of the boat with the anchor's descent before coming to a stop.

Rick stood, his wet bottom feeling what breeze that did exist. A chill ran down his spine, causing the muscles in his arms and legs to involuntarily flex.

"Oh, come on now," Kevin said. "It ain't that cold out here. Sun'll be up soon, anyhow."

Rick looked around, putting one hand on the boat's boom as he did so. It definitely didn't look like the sun was going to be coming up any time soon. The night was black, and the clouds in the wide overhead expanse were few. Although the moon wasn't full, it appeared to be. The bright white orb floating overhead in the black breadth of countless stars shined brilliant against the darkness of the waveless ocean. And it was that cold, inky darkness beating against the sides of the sailboat beneath their feet that gave Rick the creeps. Looking down into its murky sheen made him feel like they were floating on the abyss. Had it not been for the anchor that had just dropped, he could have assumed it went down for infinity, it was so black. With one gentle shove, Rick pushed the boom out as Kevin had requested. Doing this caused the boat to totter from side to side slightly.

"Easy now," Kevin scoffed. "Don't want Ol'Betsy takin' on water, do we?"

Rick looked down at the hull of the boat with wide eyes.

Kevin laughed. "Relax, man. I was just kiddin'ya."

"Yeah, yeah…." Rick waved a hand at his friend as a passing gesture. "What the heck you expect to catch with that net this early, anyhow? I know crabbin' season technically already started, but don't you think it's a little early in the year…let alone a wee-bit too close to shore for casting? You aren't going to catch much off the side of this little sailboat. Not with that, anyhow."

"Just trust me, man."

"What, like that time I was supposed to trust you when you said I'd get a peek at Tammy Hinkly's panties if I hung out under the bleachers in sixth grade?"

"Man, you're still dwelling on that?" Kevin laughed hard, his body movements rocking the boat slightly. Water splashed the sides of the boat as he did so. "How was I supposed to know that Principle Carter was walking toward us?"

"I was grounded for a month because of—"

"Whatever, man," Kevin interrupted. "To answer your question, I was out here last night. Same spot. As for what I plan on catchin'. Well, why don't we cast this-here net so you can see for yourself?"

Rick took a deep breath and watched as Kevin unrolled the casting net, getting ready to toss it overboard.

Just when Kevin was about to release the net after rearing back with it, the water at the back of the sailboat churned with a violent splash.

"See, I told you." Kevin nodded, adjusting his stance to throw the net toward the rear of the boat, over the rudder.

Rick's eyes went wide again, this time with excitement.

With a flick of the wrist and both hands forward, the net fanned out in a wide arch before slashing down over the intended location. It floated there for only a split second before sinking away.

"What is it?" Rick asked.

"Crab," Kevin smiled. "Big ones, too."

"This close to the docks?"

"Yeah, man. This year's season is going to be huge. I just know it." Kevin nodded, and both men leaned slightly over the back of the sailboat watching the water. "I have no idea why they're out this far inland. All I know is I can make a little money on the side while I wait for the job we got set up next—"

Kevin's words were cut short.

The rudder shifted violently, causing the tiller attached to it to swing hard into the man's stomach. The fierce and unexpected shove sent Kevin off balance. And before he could even utter a single tiny yelp of surprise, the silence was filled with yet again another sudden splash in the water. Only this time, it was Kevin going overboard.

"Kevin," Rick shouted, balancing himself against the sailboat as he leaned overboard to assist his friend.

Kevin almost immediately surfaced with a breathy gasp and one arm stretched out toward the boat.

"You okay?" Rick asked, reaching out to help his friend back into the boat.

"Just help me up," Kevin said and laughed.

Rick started to laugh too, but not for long. Before he had a chance to really start chuckling it up, Kevin jutted underwater and was gone.

"Crap…" Rick dropped down to one-kneed and leaned further over the edge of the boat. "Kevin!"

This time when the man resurfaced he wasn't laughing. His eyes were filled with terror. "Help me!"

He sank again.

Something was in the water. *Something* had Kevin.

"Kevin!" Rick shouted, standing to his feet unsure what he should do.

Before he could react, Kevin's arm pierced the black expanse of the sea reaching out for help. Rick grabbed him by the elbow with one gloved hand and the jacket of the forearm with the other. Ignoring the cold, murky water as it soaked through his glove, Rick pulled with all his might to help his friend back onto the boat. Rick fell backward as he did this, but something was wrong. There was no resistance. Rick fell fast and hard, tripping over the bench and almost bumping his head against the centerboard.

Panic set in.

Rick's heart pounded in his chest. He felt faint as a rush of adrenaline surged through his body with each violent shift of the sailboat, as it swayed from side to side. Water splashed into the hull, getting Rick very wet. But this wasn't what had him in shock. No, it wasn't the water splashing all around the sailboat now. It wasn't the fact that his friend still hadn't surfaced. It was the arm.

Still lying on his back, in the middle of the boat, Rick looked down at the arm clutched tightly in his grasp. It was Kevin's arm. Only, there was no Kevin. Just the torn sleeve of Kevin's jacket with the arm inside. Rick watched as blood ran down his chest from the base of the severed sleeve. The crimson flow glistened against the bright white illumination of the moon.

Rick screamed.

That's when it happened.

The sailboat began to rock even more so than before. The water on all sides of the boat roared violently like the rushing waves of a river. Blinded by fright, Rick sat up balancing himself against the gunwale on either side of the small sailboat. With his eyes focused on the splashing waves, the severed arm no longer his focus, Kevin's severed and bloodied arm slid down Rick's chest, with a dull thump as it settled at his feet.

CLICK…CLICK…CLICK…

It was climbing into the boat.

CLICK…CLICK…

Frozen in both terror and disbelief, the only thing Rick could do was stare in horror at the monstrous thing that so eagerly wanted to join him aboard Ol' Betsy. What he was looking at couldn't be real. It just couldn't. The pincer, it was massive.

CLICK...CLICK...CLICK...

Another pincer sprang up from the deep, with a rush of salty air and water. With one veracious chomp, the massive, oversized pincer latched onto the boom. The wood splintered as the monstrous burgundy claw squeezed. The boom folded, snapping in half with a loud *crack*. The mainsail flopped down wildly, part of it landing in the hull next to Rick, while the other part of it tore away, splashing into the sea as it dangled against the mast.

With splintered wood from the sailboat's boom still clutched in one pincer, the creature's upper body appeared over the ledge of the gunwale to Rick's right. As it fell forward, resting its weight on the boat's edge, the sailboat began to tip. Kevin's severed arm rolled away from Rick's feet toward the creature. The red carapace of its back was covered in pointed spikes.

CLICK...CLICK...

Rick's mind flashed to his high school prom more than twenty-five years ago. It was when his high school sweetheart had still been alive before the fire. He saw himself dancing with her once again. The feel of her supple breast against his chest, her lavender hair tickling his chin as she rested her head against his shoulder while they danced. As odd as it may seem considering the time of year, in that moment Rick felt warm.

The sudden *CLICK* was followed by a crunch that rang out in Rick's head. He was back at the boat. Only now, the thing's compound beady eyes stared right at him down into the depths of his soul.

Rick screamed, this time in pain, as the pincer pressed into his thigh like a sharpened vice grinding bone into little bits. It's wild how much the human mind and body can endure once adrenaline has started doing what it does. Rick didn't actually feel the pain until after he watched his leg get pulled away from the rest of his body, the blood leaking out as if the hull had begun to suddenly take on water.

This was it. Rick was going to die.

He tried with all he had left to bring himself back to that special place at prom.

But, before he could—

CLICK...CLICK...CLICK...

The last thing Rick saw before death took him was a massive pincer as it closed in around his head, the enveloping darkness of its girth so large that it blotted out the light of the moon.

Chapter 1

Snow-covered mountains overlooked the entire landscape.

Walter Maninko had honestly almost forgotten how beautiful his hometown really was. The smell of the salty sea air and a gentle breeze gusting against his face brought it all back now. It was surreal to think that this quaint little town could change in the fourteen years that he had been gone. He'd been kidding himself to think that it would, because it was obvious to see that nothing had changed. He could tell, even from the distant view the ferry provided of the town as it brought him closer into shore.

Nothing had changed.

Well, that's not entirely true. He had changed.

Walter Maninko was *a man* now. That wasn't the case back then, however. The last time Walter had been to Seward, he was only a few months out of high school. A little punk *know-it-all* at the age of eighteen, he had been nothing but a troublemaker with most everyone, aside from his parents *(God rest their souls),* who were ready to see him leave. So that's exactly what he had done.

Only three months away from his nineteenth birthday, Walter had packed his bags and skipped town on the first ferry that came through. With a little money in his pocket from working the docks, his backpack with a few clothes, and his laptop, Walter was out to make a name for himself. Prove to everyone that he could be a somebody unlike all the deadbeats in town. You know the types. The ones that so easily submitted to the tyranny of contentment. With their meager fishermen jobs. Coming home every day with the stench of hot, raw fish guts on their clothes. Falling into the drudgery of daily visits to the local pub because there was nothing better to do. He was better than that. And he wanted to prove it to himself.

Prove it to everyone. His dead parents. His friends. To Angela.

Hell, she probably didn't even remember his name, let alone what he looked like. And if Walter knew any better, he was more than likely about to show up to find that one of the bullies from high school turned out to become sheriff of Seward. And to make the cliché even better, Angela probably had married the dope and had three brats of her own by now. Three little miniature bully sheriffs running around in the front yard. He couldn't blame her, though. Fourteen years was a long time for anyone. A lot could happen in that amount of time.

Not wanting to think about it, Walter turned his back to Seward as the ferry brought them closer and closer to the docks. Leaning against the railing with his back to town, he looked around at the ferry's platform. He was surprised to see that he wasn't the only person headed into town this early in the morning. Considering that the sun had only been up for a few hours, eight o'clock was pretty early for the ferry to be this busy. At least, that's how he remembered it from his youth.

Birds chirped overhead.

Even though it was somewhat cloudy, the sun was bright, dancing in and out of the clouds overhead with momentary bursts of warmth against your face and back. It felt good. There were three cars on the platform. A large green Ford Ranger, a small brown Town Car, and a rusty white church van probably loaded with produce for the local market. None of them belonged to him.

Aside from himself, there were two other people out of their vehicle on the platform enjoying the view. The breeze, the sound of the ocean beating against the front side of the ferry as it pressed forward, and the sun. What Walter could only assume were a mother and her seven-to-ten-year-old daughter were only a few feet away from him doing more than just enjoying the view and the sounds of the ocean. The little girl in her bright, pink Pokémon Go winter jacket and matching shoes was holding an orange bag of Cheetos. The cartoon cheetah on the front of the bag was staring back at Walter with an enticing *thumbs up*, as if to say *"Come on, dude.... You know you want a bite."* Every few seconds the girl would sling one into the air with the flick of the wrist. The fluffy orange 'C' shaped chip didn't last long in the air before a swarm of seagulls and pelicans darted down from above in a flurry of flapping wings and anticipation. The girl giggled and laughed as she watched the birds dance overhead, fighting over the sodium-infused morsel.

The mother waved at Walter.

In his mind this was her way to signal that she realized he had been watching them. With a nod and a smile, he looked away, first down at his cell phone, which astonishingly had a strong signal, and then over the edge of the ferry at the beating waves as they crashed against its side.

Walter Maninko wasn't sure what he was going to tell everyone once the ferry docked and he started making the rounds. Since everyone his age was in their early thirties now, he assumed anyone that was off work would still be asleep or at home waiting for the pub to open that night. Everyone had understood that he'd made it to California and had become that successful screenwriter like he had planned. Yes, it was true. He did make it to California and had managed to stay there long term. But the truth was, he had done exactly what he swore he would never do; compromise. No matter how hard he tried, none of his screenplays ever sold. He was a hack. A joke. A flake in an industry flooded with dandruff. It seemed like the entire world had the same grand idea as himself. *Skip town and move to Hollywood, making big money writing scripts for the movies.*

It was an impossible market when considering the fact that your pitch was matched by more than five dozen other guys just like you with similar scripts. He had tried to get an agent. An agent wouldn't take him unless he had sold a screenplay. But he couldn't sell a screenplay, that's why he needed an agent. After a few years of failure, Walter even gave in, trying his luck at writing commercials. Sadly, that didn't get anywhere either. The closest he ever got was a call back for a Colgate toothpaste commercial he scripted. That's all it ever ended up being though, just a call. The miserable truth: calls don't pay bills.

Which is why he eventually moved out of the big city, ending up on the outskirts of Redding, California, as a sales manager for the Dollar General, of all places. Unlike his failures as a screenwriter, Walter found it rather easy to climb the ladder of success within the company, becoming a store manager only three months into the job. Turns out, most people that work for the company are just like him: people trying to make it big in Hollywood while struggling to pay the bills. A few years into the job, however, keeping shelves full and managing what few employees he was allowed to have at his store, Walter found himself no longer interested in being creative. He was burned out. All he ever really took the time to write these days was just a grocery list. And besides, as a store manager you were paid salary, which essentially meant at least sixty hours a week. No time to write anyway. That was all well and good, but when you crunched the numbers, he was essentially working for minimum wage on the salary he had with no paid overtime.

He hated his job. He hated who he had become. In truth he was no different than the deadbeats here in Seward with their fishing careers. Doing the grind and hanging out at the pub because there was nothing better to do when they weren't on the clock. Only, in California, it wasn't called the *pub*. Why get technical, though? A pub is a pub and a bar is a bar. They're both one and the same.

He was the same.

He was no different than any of the people he had left behind all those years ago. The only difference was that he had at least given it a shot. And for that he was proud. Who else in Seward could say they even gave it that much effort?

The truth was, he was tired of his life at the Dollar General, and it was time for a change.

But that wasn't the real reason he found himself back at home. It seemed that no matter how hard he tried, life wouldn't give him a break. Just when he was finally getting to know some people in Redding, his aunt passed away. They weren't really all that close. So distant, in fact, that it wasn't considered weird when he missed her funeral. No, there was only one reason he found himself on the ferry now, only minutes away from stepping foot back onto his hometown. With his aunt gone, he had no surviving relatives. This meant no one to look after his parents' property. The one-story, four-bedroom, two-bath house that sat on a quarter acre wasn't much to look at, but someone had to take care of it.

The plan was simple.

Show up, spend a month cleaning the place inside and out, and put it on the market. As soon as it sold, he would be on his way. Back to his pathetically luxurious Dollar General life in Redding, California, where he had managed to find contentment in the daily mundane, just like everyone else here in Seward, Alaska.

"Attention passengers," a static-filled voice echoed from a speaker perched above the parked vehicles on a narrow overhang railing. The voice was so garbled with the static that it was hard to make out what was actually being said. "We'll be docking in Seward in only a matter of minutes. At this time, please make your way back to your vehicles. While doing so, please have them remain parked with the emergency brake in place. Once the ferry stops and the bridge has been lowered, an attendant will be present to assist in exiting the ferry one vehicle at a time. I repeat...."

The droning static-filled voice continued to ramble on as if it were merely prerecorded, although Walter knew better. Since he had no car of his own, he remained leaning against the ferry railing while he watched the lady and her child leave the excited birds and return to their brown Town Car. It was clear to see, based on the girl's expression, that she had not been finished entertaining herself with the birds and Cheetos. Nevertheless, the insistent mother managed to get her to the car with relative ease and little complaint.

The ferry jerked slightly as it glided into place for docking. Once it was stopped and the ferry bridge began to lower, Walter Maninko stared out onto the dock, and a flood of memories rolled in from when he worked there as a teen. It hadn't all been bad. He thought of Angela and how they had said goodbye. About how he had felt about her. About how he wished she had left with him like they had planned all those years ago. He wondered if her hair was still that bright fiery red. He could smell her now, even over the powering odors of the sea and the docks. The scent of sandalwood with a faint hint of vanilla.

Walter took a deep breath and sighed.

Maybe things could be different. All he needed to do was find out where she worked and surprise her. The distant, memory-induced aroma faded, the sound of birds, and the smell of fish and the sea rushing back in.

Walter Maninko was home.

Maybe, just maybe...this town could provide more than a little bit of income from selling his parents' house. Was it possible that he might find a life for himself here once again? The more he thought about it, the more he realized the life he had back in California wasn't really all it was cracked up to be.

Picking up his backpack and sliding it over one shoulder, Walter Maninko felt hopeful for the first time in a long while.

Maybe his luck was about to change.

Chapter 2

"I don't care what he's doing, Dotty. Just get him on the phone!"

"All right, all right," Dotty, the dispatch operator for the Seward Police Department, responded. "What's so important, anyhow?"

"Don't you mind that, *now*, okay? Just tell him to call me back right away," Deputy Bart Chandler barked back over the CB radio in his pickup truck. "We have a problem, and he needs to be down here an hour ago. This is serious. Over."

"I hear you," Dotty responded, a slight huff in her voice which indicated to Bart that she was smoking in the office again, despite being told she could no longer do that. "I'll see what I can do. Over and out."

Deputy Bart Chandler clipped the CB receiver back into place on his dashboard radio and felt to make sure that his cell phone was still in his front pocket. He had tried calling the Sheriff twice in the last fifteen minutes without any response. He checked his phone again, sliding it out of his pocket just long enough to see that he hadn't missed any calls before pushing it back into place. With one swift motion, as if he had done it countless times, Bart leaned away, backing out of the passenger seat of his truck and slamming the door shut. With one hand resting on the holster of the gun strapped to his right hip, the other hand checked his pocket once more for his cell phone. It was still there. Satisfied, he started jogging back toward the bank of rocks and snow-covered sand toward the floating debris. Ol' Betsy, Kevin's sailboat was in pieces. Bits of it were scattered across the shoreline about three miles east of the Seward Docks near Marshal's Bait and Tackle. Marshal, the owner of the store, was the one that had actually called it in a little over an hour ago.

Bart looked toward the snow-covered mountains that overlooked the town, and then back at the beating water as is ran into the shoreline. Pieces of the boat were scattered everywhere, most of it was already washed up onto the snowy shore. But that wasn't the troubling part. The issue here was *where Kevin was at*, and what happened last night. They hadn't had any type of storm blow through that Bart was aware of, so what could have caused all of this to happen? He knew that Kevin liked to drink while he was out on his boat, but nothing severe enough to merit this type of damage. At the very most, Kevin might have scuffed up the sailboat against some rocks, crashing into the shore, but nothing like this.

Brent bent down, picking up a chunk of wood that was clearly the exterior side of the boat. He could make out parts of the purple lettering that read the sailboat's name. All it read was *Ol' Be*. The rest of it was torn away, mixed in with the other bits of debris either along the snow-covered shoreline or still in the ocean floating along the subtle waves.

Just as the deputy started to stand, preparing to shout out for *Kevin* in hopes that the fisherman would hear him and call out for help, his cell phone vibrated in his pocket. He didn't even give the phone time to finishing ringing the first time through before he accepted the call and had the phone to his ear.

Looking out at the shoreline of debris, Deputy Brent Chandler said, "Sheriff... you ain't goin'a believe this...."

Less than ten minutes later Sheriff Mathew Broomberg was on the scene assessing the damage with his own eyes.

The Sheriff was a short man in his late fifties standing at a measly five foot, four inches. He was a nice man for the most part, but in the ten years that he'd been Sheriff of Seward, he had some big shoes to fill. Not necessarily because the previous sheriff had done such a great job or anything. Mostly because his stature prevented a lot of the folks in town from taking him very seriously. As time went on, however, Sheriff Broomberg managed to carve a name for himself as the sheriff that *ain't got no time to be playing around*. It was his catch phrase. People of Seward learned quickly that Mathew wasn't one to mess with. He did his job and he did it well. Seward was his home, born and raised. And no one was going to take that away from him. No big time governor from New York coming in trying to change things. And definitely no talk about his height.

Absolutely, Mathew would be the first one to admit that he first went into the police force with an agenda. He had something to prove to everyone that picked on him, and thought they could abuse and use him just because he wasn't a very big man. And it was obvious to see that he had succeeded in doing just that. He worked hard to get to where he was, not by brute force or any other crooked measure. No, he had climbed up the ranks in the way everyone should, simply from the passion he had for serving his home. Making it safer. Keeping it clean. And ensuring that the frequent tourists came and went as scheduled year in and year out without incident. Sure, there was an occasional bump in the road, but Broomberg had always been level-headed and had a tendency to get the job dealt with in one manner or another.

"We've got another seven hours of daylight left," Sheriff Broomberg said very matter-of-fact. Twisting the edge of his salt-and-pepper mustache between two fingers, he said, "I want you to round up six men with Sea-Doos to comb that ocean."

Bart nodded, jotting this down on a notepad he had stashed in his back pocket. "I think it would be good if we—"

"Get a hold of Marshal over at the bait and tackle shop," Sheriff Broomberg interrupted. "He'll know some guys that can get on this right away. I want three teams starting on the eastern shoreline near the rental cabins with the bed and breakfast. I want two of them to start at the docks west of here a few miles down. And have those two teams work their way here where we'll have the other Sea-Doos. While they do that, have those other two motorboats circle this location near the debris. If Kevin is out there floating around, we are goin'a find him today."

Bart nodded, still jotting down things on his notepad.

"And one last thing." Sheriff Broomberg stepped toward the deputy, making his short stature more apparent. He looked up at Bart with his head tilted back pretty far, and said, "Get on the horn with Dotty. Have her send a few men to clean this mess up. Have her tell them I'll feed them tonight at the pub for helping out. I want this mess cleaned up before word gets out that Kevin is missing. We don't want a panic on our hands until we've gotten a grasp on the full story. Is that clear?"

"Yes, Sir." Bart put the notepad in his back pocket and started tapping the pen in his hand against his bottom lip. Looking out toward the vast expanse of the ocean with the sheriff, he said, "What a mess."

"Well, what are you waiting for, Deputy? Quit standing there and get to work."

*****

"Isn't this great?"

"You were right. This is such a beautiful place. We should live here, for real."

"You really think so?"

"Yeah, why not?"

Exiting the Glacier Guides trail headed down the coast toward Miller's Landing, close to the Seward Docks, Sam and Malinda laughed with both excitement and shortness of breath.

"It really would be cool to actually live here," Sam said, blowing foggy cold air out from his nostrils as he breathed with each step forward.

Malinda agreed, smiling at Sam as they walked side by side down the last stretch of the Glacier Guides hiking trail. As they walked, their thick parka jackets *whooshed* and *wished* with each striding swing of the arms. They were both newlyweds and in love. On vacation in Seward for their honeymoon, the couple had spent the last three weeks renting one of the log cabins attached to Ann's Bed and Breakfast on the far side of town close to the mountains. Today was their last day before they would have to pack up and head back out into the real world.

Sam's parents had spared no expense for this trip. Rather than get them something like a toaster, it was their gift to the newlywed couple. A three-week getaway of exploration, not only of one another, but of the great Alaskan outdoors. Sam and Malinda loved spending their time outside. In fact, they had met one another while hiking the Great American East Coast Appalachian Trail. Both of them had been crazy enough to go at the seven-month hike alone. And after crossing paths several times on the trail, they decided to just stick together, hiking and telling stories as they went. Those seven months turned into two years. And now, here they were as happy as the day they met.

This vacation was perfect.

In fact, when Sam suggested that they actually move to Seward, he was being serious. And Malinda knew it. This place was exciting and fresh. There was so much to see. So much to do. Sure, neither of them were used to hiking in partial snow gear, but neither of them were amateurs unfamiliar with the experience of hiking through a few inches of November snow on occasion.

Reaching the end of the trail just before it exited onto the banks of the shoreline that surrounded the Alaskan border, Sam and Malinda stopped walking and turned to enjoy the mountain view. One last long gaze before they made it back to the cabin to start packing.

They were both so enamored with the beauty and brilliance of the majestic Alaskan landscape that neither of them heard it as the massive thing crept up behind them onto the shore from the depths of the sea.

It wasn't until the thing was right behind them, its shadow looming across the base of their view, that they realized something was wrong.

Sam turned.

Malinda screeched, her high-pitched voice echoing off of the mountains in the distance.

The giant crab-thing was as tall as Sam and its spidery-like feet clattering on the ground spanned the width of a twenty-by-twenty-foot bedroom.

"What the hell?"

Those were Sam's last words as the giant crab reached out with one snapping pincer.

CLICK... CLICK... CLICK...

The giant crab's pincer engulfed Sam's torso. And with one single *crunch*, Malinda was sprayed with a red burst of crimson warmth. She just stood there screaming, her newly married husband's warm blood covering her chest and face. She watched with wide eyes of incredulity as the upper half of her husband fell away, his face frozen in terror. His face stayed frozen in that same teeth-grinding glare of disbelief as his severed upper half collapsed at her feet.

The snow around her was painted red.

The giant crab skittered toward her.

CLICK…CLICK…

It chomped its blood-soaked pincers in rapid succession as it approached her.

CLICK…CLICK…CLICK…

Malinda felt a sudden warmth in her gut as the monster stood over her. It was so warm that it burned. She felt frozen. It was like she couldn't move. She couldn't turn and run no matter how hard she tried. She fell on her side in the snow, blood starting to bubble in her throat. The burning sensation in her stomach increased as she coughed, adding to the red snow that already surrounded her.

CLICK…

Malinda did eventually die, but not before realizing that the thing standing a few feet away had been eating her severed legs.

Chapter 3

Walter Maninko sat at the narrow bar of the poorly lit pub. That was exactly what it was called too, The Pub. It was Seward's prime spot for all the happenings of the day, week, or month. From what he remembered of the place as a teen, the pub was much bigger. The stools, pool tables, and bar had been much taller. The space away from the three pool tables, the juke box, and the broken Space Invaders pinball machine was what made up more than seventy percent of the pub itself. The bar that wrapped the serving station had stools to seat an easy forty people. And from what Walter remembered of the place from back then, it had no problems doing that after dark every night of the week.

Behind him, away from the bar, there were about twenty small tables with seating for three at each table.

The tables and bar stools were weathered wood. The room smelled of stale, flat tap beer and sliced lemons. Behind the bar, a small five-by-two-foot narrow mirror lined the wall, allowing Walter to see most of the bar behind him from where he sat. The mirror itself was surrounded on all sides along that wall with a variety of liquors, wines, and assorted alcohol. Above the mirror in the same weathered wood was a framed photo of the pub from the street in black and white. People coming and going in the street dressed to match the era that the photo had been taken in, back in the early 1900s. It was a creepy photo then, and it was a creepy photo now.

Even though Walter knew that the juke box was busted, given the fact that it wasn't lit up and the glass broken out in the front, a song by the band Boston played softly through two overhead speakers at each end of the bar. It looked like the speakers were the newest thing in the entire pub. They seemed out-of-place, modern devices in a world built only for the telegram.

If you wanted to hear from some of the older men about *Killer Koala bears from another dimension*, the *Dark Man* theories, *Hitches*, or any other such conspiracy nonsense, then Glen Moore was the guy to talk to at this place. He was at the bar every night, which was surprising considering Walter remembered the guy as already being super old back when he was a kid. Even still, there was an entire group of old farts like this who lived in Seward, and practically lived at the pub. That was one of the main things aside from Angela's red hair that was hard to forget.

But none of those old guys were at the bar now. In fact, no one was. The only customer there was himself.

"You said she'll be in around six thirty?"

"Yeah, dude. Like for the third time already. She'll be in." The young guy with a hole in his right ear the size of Walter's thumb stood behind the counter. He proceeded to slide in from a row of double doors that led to the back room and dumped a bucket of ice into a vat below the bar right next to Walter. "Who did you say you were again?"

"Just an old friend, is all."

"Well, I ain't never seen you around, mister." The bar-back leaned against his empty bucket.

"Yeah, I'm just passing through." Walter stared at the massive earring in the kid's ear. It looked more like a giant hole. It wasn't that he hadn't seen that kind of thing before. He did, after all, live in California. He was just surprised to see that such a fad had made its way all the way out here. "Only going to be here for a little bit. Wanted to let her know I was going to be in town, is all."

"I can pass the message on if you want." The young bar-back put the bucket under his right arm and said, "Technically, I shouldn't have let you in here. We don't open for another forty-five minutes anyway. And until she gets here it's just me, man. Filling the kegs, taps, ice and junk. I got a lot to do. Such is the life of a bar-back." He shrugged.

Walter grinned. The kid wasn't even twenty years old yet, and he was sounding as if he was settling already. This town was a death trap and it ate up anyone it could. The grin turned into a chuckle as he sipped from the soda water that the kid behind the counter had been nice enough to give him.

"Want a refill before I go to the back? I got to start cutting up limes and lemons. Usually takes a while."

"Yeah, sure." Walter made the rest of his drink disappear with two mighty gulps before handing it over.

It tasted flat like it didn't have enough carbonation in it, but it was something to drink. And this kid had been nice enough to let him in out of the cold. Even if it was only a little after five-thirty.

The place would be opening soon. Walter thought of Angela's red hair.

"Hey, kid. Can I ask…?" Walter cleared his throat and fidgeted with the crusty looking bowl of peanuts that sat nearby on the bar. "Is she seeing anybody?"

When he looked up, the kid was already gone, his drink refilled. New chunks of ice floated at the top of his glass. He stared at them for a minute, watching them as they still spun slightly in the glass.

With both hands clasped around the cup, Walter Maninko sighed. Taking a long, generous drink, his thoughts began to wander.

There were just too many things running through his mind. Things he wanted to say. Questions he wanted answered. Questions he hoped he could answer.

Rather than focus on that, knowing that the conversation would never play out exactly how he had it planned in his head, Walter focused on all the things he needed to do with his parents' property.

He had already been by there. It had been the first stop he made after exiting the ferry that morning. The house wasn't in too bad of shape. Fix a few holes in the drywall, add a few gallons of paint, and he would be in business. The work that needed to be done on the outside was another animal altogether. The grass was overgrown. The bushes looked more like they were attempting to become trees. And the above ground hot tub that belonged to his aunt in the back yard had probably seen better days. It was a pile of junk. He already knew it was going to cost him a pretty penny to get that thing hauled away. All he had to do was figure out how it was wired in with the house and get it properly disconnected. Hopefully, the hot tub wouldn't be too much of a hassle. The yard work, on the other hand, was going to be a nightmare. He had no idea how he planned to manage the lawn when it had an easy five inches of snow already built up. In another three to four weeks, the snow would be three times as high all over town. He wished he'd thought about that before making the trip. Doing all of this during the warmer months rather than in the first part of November would have been a more ideal situation.

It was a frustrating situation.

There was nothing he could do about it now. He was already here. He just needed to get done what he could and get it sold.

Committed with the idea of waiting for Angela to show up, Walter dug his cell phone out of his front pocket. Still, full bars. Surprising. The battery, on the other hand, was cutting it close to done. He had spent too much time staring at it on the plane and the ferry. He scrolled through Facebook for a little while and checked the status on his Cthulhu virtual pet. He had a lot of gaming apps on his phone, but that one was the best in his opinion. It didn't take a lot of effort to play. And if something came up while he was in the middle of playing, it didn't really effect the game all that—

"Excuse me, but you can't be in here."

He recognized her voice right away.

"We don't open for another fifteen minutes."

The phone vanished as he slid it into the front pocket of his hefty jacket. Turning around, trying like hell not to blush, Walter was awestruck by her beauty.

"Well, if it ain't Angela C. Smith."

"Excuse me," her brow furrowed as she stepped up to the bar, dropping a purse on the stool next to Walter. "Do I know you?"

"I would hope you do," Walter said. "It's me, Walter Maninko."

Angela laughed, opening her arms to greet him. "I know who you are, silly."

They hugged for a long moment. Walter never wanted it to end. Her hair was still long and red like it had been when they were kids. She smelled wet and damp like the snow outside, but even still he could smell it beneath her thick parka.

"Sandalwood vanilla," he muttered.

"What?"

The hug ended, and they stood smiling at one another.

"Oh, nothing," he said. "How did you know it was me?"

"You mean, aside from the fact that you look exactly the same as when we were dating?"

"Yeah." Walter laughed.

Angela's shoulders bobbed slightly. "The bar-back, Mark, told me you were here already."

"Oh...."

"Why wouldn't he? A creepy looking city dweller comes into the pub nearly an hour before it opens and starts asking questions about the owner, and you think he wouldn't have made a phone—"

"Owner? No way?"

"Yes *way*." She smiled. "It's a long story."

"I want to hear all about it."

"And I'd be happy to tell it, Walter. I really have missed you." She hugged him again, his arms flapping at his waste as she did.

Walter blushed, but hoped she couldn't tell. Maybe it looked like he had just been out in the snow, is all.

"I want to hear every detail," he said. "How have you been?"

"Busy." Angela raised both arms, pointing at the building they were currently standing in. "But I can't really get into it now. Like I said, *I'm busy.*"

Walter watched her pick up her purse. "I totally understand."

"I know." She smiled. "I gotta get the pub opened up."

"What, earring boy back there can't handle it by himself?"

"Yeah." She sighed with a grin. "He's going through a phase. Like *you* never did that."

"Hey, now." Walter wagged a finger at her playfully. "Bellbottoms were never a phase, okay? I still wear those. It's my life."

"I can see that," she said, looking down at his Wrangler jeans, which happened not be bellbottoms. "Look, why don't you stick around? Have a few drinks on the house… so long as you don't make me broke."

"I'd like that."

"Good. I'm going to get things ready for tonight. Maybe after it slows down a little bit we can sit and talk. Do some catching up."

"Yeah." Walter smiled, hoping his cheeks weren't turning red. "I'd like that. I'd like that a lot."

And with that, she patted him on the shoulder and walked around the bar with her purse slung over one shoulder. Although she was wearing a heavy coat that hung down lower than her rear, Walter imagined her supple figure as he watched her walk away, disappearing beyond the swinging double doors that led into the kitchen.

Walter Maninko's stomach was tight with anticipation.

The butterflies were alive.

Chapter 4

Deputy Bart Chandler gritted his teeth with aggravation.

Having done exactly as Sheriff Broomberg had insisted, Bart went over to the Bait and Tackle shop to round up a few men who owned motorboats in an attempt to fish out Kevin's body. That is, to assume, that he was actually out there among the wreckage of his own sailboat.

Thing was, Bart didn't really understand the sheriff's logic, anyhow. He was in a hurry to find the body, sure. But that is to say, *if* there was one to be found. The reasoning seemed silly. Bart knew good and well that by this time tomorrow the entire town would have already heard the news. Kevin's sailboat was totaled and washed up along the shore near Mathew's bait store. And if the entire town was going to know about that, then they would sure find out about the body, or lack thereof.

So, why the hush? It just didn't make sense to try keeping something like this low key.

In Bart's mind, if the Sheriff wanted to find the body floating in the wreckage across the shore before dark, it would have been easier to do with more help than just a few Sea-Doos. If everyone was already going to find out, then just have everyone help conduct the search and be done with it. It was too cold to be out here doing this kind of thing at sundown. If he had more help they would have already been done. But, no one ever asked him. Who was he to know any better? He was just the lowly old deputy and nothing more. Everything the sheriff said was the golden truth of verbal law. Bart's suggestions, on the other hand, just a passing fart in the wind. If the Sheriff didn't say it, then it wasn't a good idea.

All Bart needed to do was bide his time until the short-order-giver retired. Maybe then, Bart would have his chance to be the one calling the shots and always interrupting people when they have suggestions.

Flip the script.... Yeah, he liked the sound of that.

Bart stood outside his truck leaning against the grill with both shoulders resting on the hood. Next to him sat a steaming cup of coffee that he had picked up from the Bait shop while rounding up some men to scavenge the coastline. With his truck parked in the parking lot of the bait shop, he used his binoculars to scan the shoreline from where he stood. From where he was parked, the snow-covered beach was less than a quarter acre from his location to the crashing waves. It was a good spot to post a lookout. He was close enough to the beach that he could run out to the men in the motorboats if they found something. And close enough to his truck, that if it got too cold, he could crank her up and sit inside for a little warmth.

Sheriff Broomberg, on the other hand, had it easy, as always. After swinging by Kevin's house to make sure he wasn't just sitting up in bed or watching TV, he had nothing else really to do. With no luck there, he was probably already back at the station sitting in his chair, enjoying the heat of his office. Doing nothing but waiting on the phone to ring with news from Bart that Kevin had been found.

Bart rolled his eyes at the thought, taking a sip from his steaming coffee. It felt good in the palm of his gloved hands.

In total Bart had managed to wrangle up a whopping ten men with the help of Mathew at the bait and tackle shop. As the Sheriff had requested, they had two Sea-Doos on the east side near the hiking trails and cabins, two more on the west side near the docks, and two within binocular view from Bart near the boat wreckage. With one man in each motorboat, that left four guys that had been nice enough to leave the comfort of their warm homes to help clear the wreckage from the beach. These men were working in two teams of two, picking up chunks of the boat, and gathering them all together in one location for easy pick-up the next morning.

Two of the men were within view close enough that they would probably hear him if Bart decided to shout something. The other two men had started in the same spot as the others, but had managed to walk down the shoreline a ways toward the west in the direction of the docks. In his binoculars, Bart saw them and the pile they were making from the debris, but even then they were still pretty small.

What mattered was that *the mess was getting picked up*.

Sadly, though, no sign of Kevin…yet.

It was coming up on six thirty and they were losing sunlight. If they were going to find something significant it needed to happen in the next few minutes for multiple reasons. Reason one, they weren't going to get much done in the dark. And two, the pub was about to open, which meant these men were probably just as ready to be done with the search as Bart was.

The sun had already set. The sky was filled with dark purples and faint pinks. What few clouds were in the sky were moving slowly, which meant it wasn't too windy. This was a good thing considering the time of year. Those men were probably miserable picking up all that boat rubble with wet hands. But it had to be done.

Bart took another sip from his coffee, letting the steam rise up. As the heat rose around his face, it only helped as a reminder of how cold his cheeks really were. It felt good, but his face would be just that much colder when he finished the drink and found himself standing around with nothing warm to hold.

As he started to take another sip, his phone vibrated in his front pocket.

Setting the cup down on the hood of his truck, he retrieved the phone and accepted the call. It was Juan, one of the men in the Sea-Doos on the east side of the shoreline near the cabins.

"Deputy Chandler," Bart said. "Please tell me you found something, Juan."

"Help us! Oh my God!" The phone thudded as if Juan dropped it.

"Juan…Juan!" Bart stepped away from his truck. "Juan…. Hello!"

The call disconnected.

Before Bart could try calling him back, it happened.

The first few Alaskan King Crab that appeared on the shoreline were of average size. First there was one. And then four. The men working on collecting rubble and debris were just as stunned as Bart. He had never seen anything like it. King Crab was a deep sea catch.

What in the hell are they doing this far in, let alone coming ashore like that? Bart thought, watching their numbers grow from four to a dozen or more.

"Holy crap, Stewart!" one of the men manning a Sea-Doo close to the shoreline near Bart shouted out.

The deputy brought his binoculars to his face and looked out. One of the two men on the motorboats was missing. The motorboat was just floating there in the water, unmanned. The other guy on the other boat was standing, panicked, as he kept scanning the water around his boat.

That was when Bart watched it happen in all its magnified glory.

The man standing in his Sea-Doo scanning the water was suddenly grabbed, and then was gone. It happened so fast Bart wasn't sure what he was seeing. It was just a massive splash of water, something red, and then the guy was gone. The two Sea-Doos were empty, just out in the water floating all alone.

Another scream came, this time faint, and from the west.

With the binoculars still pressed against his eyes, Bart scanned the horizon toward the west. One of the men that had been off in the distance collecting bits of the wreckage was running toward him. The other man that had been with him wasn't anywhere to be seen.

Instead, Bart was looking through his binoculars at a monstrosity. There were dozens of little average-sized king crab skittering on the snowy banks of the beach, but that wasn't all. A monstrous-sized crab that looked like it could have been bigger than Bart's truck was in hot pursuit. Unlike the smaller crabs that skittered in a sideways pattern, this giant one was clomping headlong toward its prey and gaining ground.

Bart couldn't believe what he was seeing. And he didn't even realize it until it was already happening, but his binoculars were done and his gun was unholstered as he shouted for the man to keep running toward him.

Bart shot two rounds toward the creature, his pistol buckling slightly with each gentle squeeze. The thing wasn't even fazed. It just kept on coming.

CLICK...CLICK...CLICK...

Bart adjusted him aim, but before he could take another shot at the creature, a set of screams came from nearby out on the beach.

Frantic, Bart craned his neck toward the abandoned motorboats, and the two men standing on the beach collecting bits of wreckage. Only, those two men were *no longer alone*.

A giant crab rushed up onto the shore with both enormous pincers chomping with excitement.

CLICK...CLICK...

One of the men slipped as the creature fell on him, its giant pincers meeting him headlong with one violent *snip*. In a gush of crimson spray, as if the man had been a water balloon filled with red Kool-Aid, the snow-covered beach was stained with his insides as intestines and viscera splashed out. When the two pincers came apart, so did the man. His head and arms fell to one side in the snow-covered sand, while his legs fell limp where they stood. His severed torso began being devoured by the giant thing.

"Holy hell!" Bart fired his pistol wildly in rapid succession. "This can't be happening."

TICK...TICK...TICK.... The gun was empty. Bart stared down at it with defiance as if the gun had somehow let him down.

Bart looked to his right, momentarily forgetting about the man that had been getting chased. The man was gone. All that remained was a giant king crab and blood-stained snow. The crab was standing in place, chomping chunks of bloodied meat into its mandibles. Its beady eyes on either side of its chomping mouth darted erratically in all directions. Around it, tons of smaller, normal-sized Alaskan king crab skittered around frantically on the snowy beach.

It wasn't until Deputy Bart Chandler was in the truck slamming the door that he saw three more giant crabs surface among the crashing waves.

This just can't be happening. This can't be real.

Bart's heart pounded in his chest. His hands shook, and this time not from the cold.

With the key in place and his foot on the gas, the truck's wheels spun in place before catching traction. When they did catch tread, the truck jerked back, sending Bart suddenly in reverse. Panicked, he hit the brake, but not before backing into the handicap access sign in the bait and tackle parking lot. The sign bent back hard, falling to the parking lot gravel. Bart jammed the truck into drive and stared out at the beach one last time. The shoreline was littered with averaged-sized king crabs. But that wasn't the thing that had his heart ready to burst from his ribcage.

There was an easy five or six giant crabs on the snow-covered beach making their ways toward him. And from the looks of it, they weren't alone.

Bart hit the gas and spun out before driving off, sending bits of the parking lot gravel up into the air.

The deputy watched in his rearview mirror as five or six giant crabs became a dozen.

The beach was alive with ten-legged terrors.

Chapter 5

Walter couldn't help but chuckle at least a little. This place hadn't changed a bit. It was only a little after six-thirty and the pub was already starting to fill up. The sun was down. It was getting dark. And a little more than half of the barstools were being warmed by the butt cheeks of fishermen, fishermen's wives, and dock hands alike.

The pub smelled like the salt of the ocean and raw fish guts.

Surprisingly, Walter didn't mind the smell. In fact, in a way it was nostalgic. It reminded him of his youth, working the docks, and playing pinball and pool at the pub after work.

The pub was noisy.

Walter sat alone in the back corner at one of the round tables with three chairs. He was shocked to see that no one had walked up to greet him, considering the number of people already seated, drinking, and telling stories. He attributed this to the idea that maybe he didn't look like he used to. No one recognized him. And honestly, he liked it that way. So far, there no one had arrived worth talking to, anyhow, with the exception of Angela. But she had been too busy running things, filling drinks, making calls, and taking orders for the kitchen.

Walter liked watching her work.

When Angela wasn't out on the floor dealing with drunkards and customers alike, Walter found himself staring at his cell phone. He occasionally refreshed his Facebook feed, finding nothing of interested. But mostly he spent his time playing Cthulhu Virtual Pet. It was a fun simple game that was easy to look away from when Angela appeared behind the bar or out on the floor talking to customers near the pool tables.

She was beautiful.

Even more so than when they were teenagers. She had definitely filled out, which was easy to see now that she didn't have that large parka on, hiding her tight jeans and the deep V-neck t-shirt. The dark purple shirt made her long, fiery red hair stand out even in the dim pub lighting.

Walter tried to be inconspicuous while he watched her work, but the occasional glance and subtle smile that she gave him only reinforced the idea that she knew he was watching.

Walter only hoped that she didn't mind. It was hard to read what the smile actually meant, but he hoped that it meant she was also interested in what might have been had he not moved away.

Angela disappeared back into the kitchen through the swinging double doors.

As he had done countless times in the last half an hour, Walter sighed and looked back down at his phone.

"Hey buddy, I see what you're doin'."

Walter didn't look up, his focus on feeding his virtual underwater god.

"Hey, pal." A man slammed his hand down on Walter's table. "I'm talkin' to you."

"What?" Walter looked up with surprise.

"Yeah, that's right. I see you eyein' Ms. Angela every time she comes out of that-there kitchen."

"Hey man, it isn't like th—"

"I wasn't done talkin' to you."

Walter sized up the man, setting his phone down on the table. The man was probably just shy of six-foot. One hundred and ninety pounds. Unlike Walter, who slung a cash register for a living, this guy probably slung bait and mainsail lines for a living. He didn't look big, but it was safe to assume the man was in much better shape.

"Listen here, mouth breather. We don't take kindly to strangers. And we definitely don't take kindly to strangers eyein' up the locals."

"Mark, would you shut up and leave that man alone," someone called from across the bar. "Do you even know who that is?"

"What the hell do I care?" the man standing over Walter said. "Looks like *trouble* to me."

"Show some respect," the voice called out again. "That's the Maninko family's boy. He's in town settling their estate now that the last of the Maninkos is dead. Hell, you two went to high school together."

Walter smiled, looking past the man before him, but still not getting a good look at who had been talking.

"Well, ain't that just beat all." The man smiled, pulling up a chair and sitting with Walter at the table. "Walter Maninko, as I live and breathe."

"That's me," Walter said. "And you must be Mark."

Mark nodded, slapping his hand on the table again.

A waft of salty fish odor glided off the table, insulting Walter's nostrils.

"Is this guy bothering you?" Angela stepped up to the table, an empty tray balanced in one hand. With her other hand resting on Walter's shoulder, she said, "Mark, you behave. I plan on having dinner with this man later tonight. So, don't you go scaring him off…okay?"

Mark blushed, his eyes locked on what lie between the slit in her purple V-neck shirt while running his fingers through his hair.

"I'll behave," he said.

"Can I get you boys anything to drink?" Angela took out her notepad. "We've got a dozen oysters, buy one, get another half-dozen free."

"No thanks," Walter said. "Don't want to ruin my appetite. Saving it for a date I've got later on tonight."

He felt like an idiot saying it, but it was too late. The words had already come out of his mouth. But somehow, when he looked up at Angela to try gauging her reaction to the statement, all she did was smile at him.

Walter's stomach churned, and he hoped he wasn't blushing.

"No food for me." Mark belched. "What I will have is another brewski."

Angela nodded, turning toward the bar, and walking away. Both men watched her hips and those tight jeans as she went. Only difference was, Mark's eyes were wide and his mouth hung open.

"Boy, let me tell you." Mark wiped drool from his mouth. With a grunt, he said, "That girl is the cream of the crop. Too bad what happened to her old man."

Walter's brow creased as he leaned forward in his chair. "Old man?"

"Yeah," Mark said, "He was...."

Angela stepped up to them again, setting a pint of beer on the table in front of Mark. The white foam floated on the top perfectly for only a few seconds before sliding to one side spilling down the side of the glass. Walter watched as the foam soaked into the table.

Mark looked up at her and smiled, but not before picking up his beer and glancing at her cleavage.

"Thank you, kindly."

"Tab?"

"Yes, indeedy." Mark smiled again, this time bringing the glass to his lips, most of the foam that was left spilling down into his lap.

Walter watched with amazement as the man sitting with him proceeded to down the entire pint in one glorious gulp after another. He didn't manage to drink it all, but by the time Mark set the glass back down on the table, it only had a few sips left floating at the bottom.

Now that Angela was gone, Mark cleared his throat, and whispered, "It's a true shame. It really is. To only be married to that fella for a few years and him end up lost at sea like that. Fell overboard during a crabbing job. Weather got real bad. I was part of that crew, too. Real scary stuff."

"Wow," Walter said, looking away from Mark toward the bar, but Angela wasn't in view.

"That ain't even the worst of it neither." Mark picked up his glass, preparing to finish it off, but then said, "That girl of hers is goin'a have to grow up without a daddy. That's tough business. It really is."

"Daughter?"

"Yeah, Angelina. Named after her mama. Only, most everyone around here calls her *Lina* for short."

"How old is she?" Walter probed.

"Oh, I don't know," Mark said, downing the last of what beer was left in his glass. Once he set it back down on the table empty, he said, "Maybe five or six, if I had to guess. Angela got pregnant pretty much right after they got married. Big gossip of the town for a while was whether or not she got pregnant before the wedding. But I don't know. It don't rightly matter no more. What matters is, *Lina*. So, I don't take too kindly to people eyeing her mama's bits…if you know what I mean?"

"Yeah, I know what you mean." Walter rolled his eyes. *All you've been doing since you got here is eye her bits,* Walter thought.

"Man, that's got to be tough," Walter said. "How does she find the time to own and operate the pub with her kid at home?"

"Beats me," Mark said. "Say…I remember you now. You're *the* Walter Maninko. You and Angela used to date when we was in school."

"Yeah, that's me."

"No wonder you're sittin' here all creepy-like. You tryin' to make you some moves on the old lady?"

"No, I'm doing no such thing," Walter said. *Or am I?*

Mark started to ask him if he wanted to join him at a game of pool, but Walter's mind was elsewhere, focused on all the details that had just been provided to him by this bumbling idiot. Angela was a widow. She had a five-or-six-year-old kid. She owned the pub. It appeared that she'd had no problem moving on with her life after he went away. But who was he to blame her? It had been more than ten years. Of course she had moved on.

"Hey, man." Mark waved his hand in Walter's face. The air was suddenly filled with the pungent odor of piss and fish. And just as quickly, it subsided when Mark pulled his hand away. "You even listenin' to me? Want'a play some pool?"

"Yeah, sure." Walter started to stand. "Why not?"

But before he could even get out from under the table all the way, the front door to the pub swung open. Cold air rushed into the room. The old man standing in the doorway was shriveled in stature. Probably in his late seventies, the man was hunched over slightly, with liver spots on his hands and his balding scalp. Despite his size and age, the man was pretty spry. In one quick motion, he spun around slamming the door shut with frantic abandon.

"Oh, dear God!" the old man shouted. "We have to hide, now!"

"Calm down, old man," someone said. "Sit down and have a pint."

This merited laughter from most of the patrons in the pub.

"Shut up and listen," the old man insisted, shouting over the mockery and mirth. "Monsters, I tell you. Tons of them coming out of the water. And they're headed this way. We have to do something, now!"

"What the hell are you going on about?" Mark stepped away from Walter and toward the front of the pub. "You been on that *toot* again, old man?"

"No, I ain't on no *toot*," the old man demanded. "They're coming. Turn off the lights. We can't let them know we're in here."

Mark went to the window, with everyone in the pub watching on. "There ain't no monsters after you, old man. Just like there ain't no *Dark Man* in your closet or *green men* landing in your backyard in them silver disks. Okay?"

"What's the matter, Mr. Glen?" Angela was at the front door pulling Glen Moore toward the bar to have a seat. "Let's get you calmed down so you can tell us exactly what is going on, okay?"

"We don't got no time for that." Glen Moore pulled away from Angela. "They're dead. They're all dead."

Chapter 6

"I'm sorry, but there is no way in the world that giant crabs are attacking the city."

"I don't care if you believe me or not," old man Glen Moore argued. "I just came in to warn everyone. Now, if you don't mind, I'll be on my way."

But before he could push past Mark, Angela, Walter and a few of the other pub patrons, one of the windows near the front door ruptured in a fury of shattered glass, cold air, and something red and scaly.

"What the hell was that?" Mark stepped back, distancing himself from the window.

A giant red crab pincer jammed its way through the opening where the broken windowpane once was.

"Holy crap!" someone shouted as the bar became a room filled with the chaos of confusion and disbelief.

CLICK...CLICK...CLICK...

The pincer gnashed at the cold air inside the pub, trying to get at anything that dared get too close.

"There's more of them!" a woman shouted from her hiding place ducked low behind one of the pool tables.

When Walter looked toward the window that she had been pointing at, his eyes went wide with horror. More than a dozen Alaskan king crabs dashed across the parking lot and street out in front of the pub. But that wasn't what had his jaw dropped, his body frozen in bemusement. There were several crabs among the many that were enormous. Most of the larger ones were bigger than a truck or van. There was just no way that this could actually be happening.

"I'll take care of this," Mark said, obviously not aware of the many that were lingering in the streets outside. "Ain't nothin' but a giant crab. I catch these sons-a-bitches for a livin'."

"What are you going to do?" Angela asked, panic in her shivering voice.

"You still got that shotgun behind the bar by the register?"

She nodded.

With that, Mark darted around the bar to retrieve the shotgun.

"I don't believe this," Walter said, locking gazes with Angela.

Then, as if somehow Walter had suddenly taken off the muffs from his ears, sound rushed back into his senses. People were screaming and shouting, both at one another, and at the creatures outside. The pub was in a panic. Someone ran past him with his arm missing. Blood sprayed from the missing appendage as he darted by. Blood soaked the pub floor at Walter's feet. There was so much shouting and screaming that it was just one big noise.

"Move!" Mark shouted, stepping in front of the busted window and the large pincer jutting from it into the pub. He lifted the shotgun toward the window and shouted, "Go to hell!"

The loud shotgun blast reverberated off the pub walls. Walter's ears rang as he watched the shotgun jolt in Mark's hands.

The giant pincer in the window vanished.

"That'll show you," Mark said, but then it happened.

The giant crab that had been blocking the window was replaced by a swarm of smaller, average-sized Alaskan king crab. The red crabs flooded the window opening, pouring into the pub like sand spilling out of one side of a broken hourglass.

Mark fired the shotgun again.

This time it didn't seem as loud because Walter had been expecting it, and because his ears were still ringing.

The shotgun kicked a third time in the fisherman's hands, but they just kept coming.

"There's too many of'em." Mark aimed to fire a fourth time.

That was when Walter finally snapped into action, no longer frozen with confusion and doubt.

"We've got to get the hell out of here." Walter grabbed Angela by the arm, who also seemed to be in just as much shock as himself, and turned toward the double doors leading into the kitchen.

She didn't resist and was easily led back behind the bar. As Walter pulled her to safety, he watched in his peripheral as the carnage ensued. To his left, near the pool tables, a man was getting jumped by two smaller crabs. His screams were drowned out by the panic of everyone else around him. Beyond the man being attacked, a group of five bar patrons huddled down behind one of the pool tables, watching with wide horrified eyes. As Walter made it around the bar with Angela in tow, he caught a glimpse of himself in the reflection of the large black-and-white picture that hung above the bar. He, too, had that same *wide eyes, panic-filled expression* plastered across his face.

Walter ducked down behind the bar, pulling Angela down with him.

The shotgun rang out again, and this time, it sounded like Mark had started screaming in pain. But then again, it could have been anybody. The entire pub was one giant scream of sudden and unexpected chaos.

"Angela, we've got to move." Walter shook her by the shoulders. "Snap out of it. We've got to go."

Angela shook her head, and the glazed expression in her eyes seemed to subside. "We've got to go," she agreed.

"Yes, we do," Walter demanded. "Now, come on…do you have a car? Please tell me you have a car."

"A car…a car. Yes, yes…I have a car," she said, obviously still in shock from what was happening around them.

"We need to leave," Walter said, continuing to shake her.

Blood sprayed out over the bar where they were hiding and rained down on them in a light, warm silky drizzle of crimson.

The sound of clamping claws and clattering crab feet dashing across the pub's wooden floor filled the air amidst the screams.

Walter willed himself to give one quick glance. When he did, he saw a lady being chased by a crab. A giant crab claw jutting from the busted window clamped tightly around one of the bar tables. The shotgun was on the floor by the front door in a pool of blood. The only remnants of Mark that Walter could see was one shoe sitting on the floor a few steps away from the shotgun. And it looked like there might still be a foot inside. Blood pooled out from the severed limb onto the pub's old, weather-beaten wood floor.

Something slammed hard against the front door of the pub.

CLICK... CLICK... CLICK...

Whatever it was, it was big. The *boom* came again, and from what he could see, Walter knew that that front door wasn't going to hold for much longer.

"Your car, Angela. Your car."

"Right, my car," she said, this time seemingly with more self-control. "My jacket. My keys are in my jacket."

She pointed beyond Walter toward the far side of the bar closer to where he had been sitting. Without hesitation, Walter shimmied his way down the side of the bar without poking his head up to take a look. It wasn't until he was almost at the end of the bar that he saw it. Her coat was hanging on a rack near the register. In order to get to it, he would have to expose himself momentarily above the bar.

The loud *boom* came again at the front door. Only this time the sound was followed by splintering wood, and the separation of hinges and paneling. Whatever wanted in sounded like it was definitely making an entrance.

It was now or never.

Walter Maninko jutted up from the confines of his hiding space behind the bar and grabbed Angela's parka off the rack. And just as quickly he ducked back down out of view, but not before taking in some of the carnage.

For starters, his cell phone was still sitting on the table too far away now to reach. He had left it there when the old man, Glen Moore, had charged in blabbing on about what ended up being the truth. The few people that had been hiding behind the pool tables were now in an all-out war with the smaller crabs. They were cornered, and there was only so much that cue balls and pool sticks could do.

One man swung the pool stick hard, connecting headlong with one of the creatures. The creature flew across the top of a pool table, colliding with the wall on the other side. Unfortunately, it was up and back in pursuit just as quickly as it had hit the wall.

The entrance to the pub was a bloodbath of chaos. Arms, legs, and even heads littered the floor. A string of intestines that started in the center of the room appeared to lead in a slippery visceral trail outside into the parking lot, where Walter could hear people running and screaming. The doorway, or lack thereof, was a wide open mess of splintered wood and bent boards. The door itself was gone. What stood in its wake was one of the giant crab still just a little too big to squeeze through. That didn't mean it wasn't trying. The giant monster pressed against the pub entrance, its pincers slamming the opening wider with each fervent blow.

CLICK...CLICK...

"Got the jacket." Walter gasped, scooting back toward Angela, who was still ducked down behind the bar.

She reached into the parka jacket pocket to reveal a set of keys, with a keychain framed photo the size of a quarter. Walter didn't get a good look at it, but the photo looked like it might be that of a little girl.

"Here, put this on," Walter said, handing her the coat as he darted past her toward the double doors leading into the kitchen. "It's going to be freezing cold out there."

Angela took the jacket, sliding into it fairly quickly. With the car keys in hand, she signaled with a nod that she was ready to get the hell out of there.

Walter's heart sank seeing the look of anguish and terror stricken across her beautiful face. But he couldn't think of that now. He needed to focus.

With one glance at the double doors, Walter craned his neck toward the chaos that was taking place in the pub. He looked back at the double doors. This was it. Walter took Angela by the hand and forced the first step forward.

His grip on Angela was tight as they darted out from behind the bar and through the double doors into the kitchen. As the doors swung closed behind them, one of the smaller crabs gave chase. It jumped on Walter, knocking him to the ground. Its pincers snapped furiously at Walter's face, but he managed to keep them at bay with his elbows up. One of the pincers clamped onto his forearm—hard. Walter screamed. He could feel the warmth of blood as it filled in the sleeve of his winter jacket.

Angela screamed, lunging forward with a large frying pan. With one wild swing, the creature was off of Walter and upside down on the floor. But Angela didn't stop there. She just kept swinging. The sound of metal slamming against the tiled kitchen floor echoed off the stainless steel appliances.

Walter stood there watching her while he cradled his arm, the creature being pulverized one solid swing at a time.

"That's enough," he said. "It's dead. It's dead."

Angela stopped swinging. Breathing heavily, she dropped the skillet beside the immobilized creature. It *clanged* as it fell to the floor before coming to rest beside the dead thing.

"Why the hell is this happening?" she said and panted.

"I'll tell you why," old man Glen Moore said, startling both of them to near-panic. Glen Moore stepped up to them from behind the kitchen prep area with a wet mop in hand, as if ready to swing it. "They're here because we brought them here. We caused this. It's our fault this is happening."

"I don't care whose fault it is," Walter said, taking Angela by the hand once more, forgetting about the throbbing pain in his forearm. "All I care about is going somewhere else. Preferably somewhere they're not." Looking toward Angela, he said, "Are you okay to drive? I don't really have much experience with driving in the snow."

She took a deep breath and nodded.

"Wherever you're headed, I want to come." Old man Glen Moore dropped the wet mop. "This pub has been overrated for years anyway."

"Then what are we waiting on?" Walter said. "Let's go."

As they reached the back door to the kitchen leading to the employee parking area, old man Glen Moore asked where they planned to go. Angela didn't hesitate in the slightest.

"Home," she said. "My girl is at home. Lina needs me."

Chapter 7

The giant crabs and their smaller counterparts came ashore all along the coastline of the Seward, Alaska, banks. In droves, they rushed the snow-covered beaches headed inland. For every thirty average-sized Alaskan king crab that made its way onto the shores there was at least one giant among them.

Although many easily found their way up the hiking trails toward the log cabins and the bed and breakfasts, most were headed toward the center of town, drawn by the commotion of activity already stirred up, by the wave of creatures who had already arrived before them.

It was the noise.

The vibrations.

They could feel it in the ground.

The sensations that ran up their exoskeleton covered, spider-like legs, sent them toward the action. It sent them toward the screams.

Toward the feeding.

The hunger drove them forward.

Although most of the crabs were headed toward the pleasures of feasting, some of the crabs, both giant and small, were headed toward the southeastern-most part of the town, drawn by a very different sort of rumbling. A type of rumbling that was faint, and distant, and yet...still called to them. Fed on their senses, urging them to investigate.

Therefore, it was no surprise when a substantial number of these creatures eventually reached the Fort Raymond Company Substation.

The Raymond Company Substation was a division of the power plant for the surrounding county. With mountains and vast valleys between each town associated with Raymond County, each town had its own separate substation which provided electricity to that particular district of the county. The Fort Raymond Company Substation for Seward was positioned on exactly two acres. Both of these acres were fully fenced-in to keep out any vandals and wildlife that may unintentionally interfere with the generators. Along with the generators, the fenced area housed a small shed for repair tools and two repair vehicles. In total, there were ten generators. Only eight of these generators ran at a given time, leaving the other two as primary backup in the event of unforeseen conditions such as bad weather, flooding, or simple generalized servicing issues.

Although the fencing that lined the two-acre plot was strong enough to keep out deer and pesky animals like raccoons, it did very little to perturb the giant crabs that so eagerly wanted to get at whatever it was causing the vibrations in the ground.

It did stop them for a moment, but within minutes of arrival, a large portion of the fence was down, folded flat against the earth, both cut up and bent to hell.

The crabs were in.

Seward's Fort Raymond Substation had been compromised.

Had someone been there to watch, they would have been witness to a spectacle of a show. But no one was there to see it. Giant crabs and small crabs alike joined in a ravenous battle of electricity against pincers and strength in numbers.

The grounds of the Fort Raymond Substation lit up in a flurry of implosions and explosions. White light sparked and danced as lines were severed and giant crabs erupted in smoke and fire.

The battle raged on, the electricity dealing an equal measure of damage to its aggressors.

Chapter 8

Deputy Bart Chandler stood in the police station lobby awestruck by the sound of ringing phones and Dotty's frantic attempt to keep up when the power went out.

"Hello," Dotty said and took a deep breath with one phone to her ear, a cigarette butt dangling from the corner of her mouth. "Hello…."

Bart watched as she tapped the old-style receiver a few times.

"No dial tone," she said, hanging up the phone. Dumping the spent cigarette into an ashtray and pulling a fresh one from her purse, she looked up to the stunned deputy. "Please tell me it ain't true. Phones been off the hook for the last forty-five minutes straight. I had all of our first responders on calls within the first three minutes. Including support from the fire station. Please tell me this is just an elaborate prank."

Dotty pulled back her disheveled hair and lit her new cigarette while Deputy Bart cleared his throat.

"It's real," he said, staring back at her in the dark. "Seen it with my own eyes. Lost all of the search crew combing the beach."

"And the Sea-Doos?" Sheriff Mathew Broomberg's voice reached across the darkness.

"Those too," Bart replied, looking toward the sheriff's office. With his eyes still adjusting to the darkness, he could see the silhouette of the short man in the doorway leading into Broomberg's office. "Saw it with my own eyes. Even unloaded a clip into one of the bigger ones. Didn't even slow it down."

"Shit…"

"What are we goin'a do?" Dotty puffed on her cancer stick, the red and orange embers bright in the darkness of the police station lobby. "I sent all those men out to what I thought was just some type of flash-mob prank."

"First of all," Bart clarified. "A flash mob is when people dance in public. This…this would be a prank of conspiracy-type proportions."

"I don't know," she said. "I just thought that maybe the entire town as plannin' one over on us for giggles, is all."

"Well, that ain't the—"

"Would you two shut up?" Sheriff Mathew stepped toward them. "Now is not the time to be goin' on like this about *Internet lingo* and *Glen Moore*-type conspiracies. If this thing is real like you say it is, Bart, then we need to do something about it. How many did you say came up out of that water?"

"I don't know," he said, a waver in his voice. "A dozen or so."

"Well, that don't sound right to me based on the calls we was gettin'," Dotty said. "We've been gettin' calls from as far as the east is from the west all across Seaward. All along the coast and as far inland as Sixth Street."

"Sixth Street?" Bart's heart skipped a beat. "That means there's too many for us to do anything with the resources we have."

Sheriff Mathew Broomberg cleared his throat as if to mock the obvious understatement.

"Then what do you propose we do, sheriff?" Bart somewhat recoiled from his own words. He had never barked back at the Sheriff like that before. But somehow, it felt right. It felt good. It felt empowering. "We can't just sit here in the dark and do nothing. We need to get a hold of the county. Have them send in some sort of reinforcements."

"Reinforcements…reinforcements?" Sheriff Mathew slammed his hand down hard on Dotty's desk. Dotty jumped in her seat. "What the hell do you think I been doin' for the last hour? Sittin' on my hands? I haven't been able to make an outgoing call to save my life. The lines have been jammed with the flood of incomin'. You heard'em yourself."

"Then what about now…let's call somebody now."

Sheriff Mathew laughed hard, rearing his head back with both hands on his belly. "Call them now? Are you really that dense, Deputy? How the hell do you expect me to call them now? The power's out, if you haven't noticed."

"Well, then, why don't we—?"

The Sheriff laughed again. "Why don't we, what? I can't wait to hear what dense idea you have now."

"No offense, Sheriff Broomberg, but you can go suck an egg." Even in the darkness of the lobby, Bart could tell that his superior had been taken aback by that statement. It felt good to start standing up for himself. "No offense, sir. But all you ever do is interrupt me. Don't get me wrong. I understand. You have a power complex. You always have. It's because of your height. But, now isn't the time to play *power trip*. Now's the time to come together with whatever ideas we've got. And so far, I haven't heard any from you."

"Do you even know who you're—?"

"Excuse me," Bart interrupted, noticing in his peripheral that Dotty's eyes were wide as she watched this conversation unfold. "But, I think the question here is *do you*? Do you know who you're dealing with out there? I saw those things for myself firsthand. If what Dotty said is true, then there is a hell of a lot more of them than just what I saw. The entire town is under siege. The town needs us, and all you're worried about is *whose word is the upper hand* in this little conversation."

"Well, then…." The sheriff cleared his throat. "What do you have in mind?"

Bart half expected the Sheriff to jam protocol and rank down his throat. But he didn't. The unexpected response left Bart in blundered silence for a moment.

"Well…?" The sheriff crossed his arms, looking up at Deputy Bart Chandler.

"How long until the backup power kicks on in the basement?"

"Depends," Dotty said. "In the summertime it would'a kicked on already. The colder it gets the longer it takes for them to kick on. Another hour, maybe."

"Then I say we wait." Bart pulled his pistol from his holster and dispensed the empty magazine. Pocketing the used magazine, he retrieved a fresh one from his belt and slid it into place. It *clicked* as he jammed it home. Satisfied, he said, "We go down in the basement, unlock the reserves, and get ready. And until the backup power kicks on, we wait."

"Wait for what?" Dotty asked.

"We wait for war."

"And when the power comes back on?" Sheriff Mathew said, checking the rounds in his revolver.

"We get on that phone and we call County. We call anyone that will help. The FBI. The CIA. The NSA. Everyone...hell, we'll even call NASA. I don't care. Just so long as we can get some people in here to help this town."

Sheriff Mathew Broomberg nodded. "I'll be right back. Let me get the key to the reserves safe. We'll all go together."

And with that, Deputy Bart Chandler led as all three of them made their way down into the basement.

With each downward step forward it got a little colder.

With the power out, it was going to be much colder very soon.

Chapter 9

With Angela behind the wheel of her red Honda Civic, and old man Glen Moore in the passenger seat, Walter Maninko pressed both hands hard for support. With one hand against each front seat, he steadied himself as Angela zigged and zagged through the suburban terrain of Seward, Alaska. The back seat was cramped, toys and children's clothing piled up at his left, and boxes of board games and puzzles stacked up on his right. Frantic to just get into her car so that they could leave, he had simply climbed into the back seat from the front before letting old man Glen Moore snag shotgun seat.

Glen and Angela were buckled in.

Walter was not.

With every sharp turn that she took, either left or right, he found himself sliding into clothing and games.

It had only been a minute since the street's power had failed. No streetlights to guide their path. No traffic lights to keep people safe. It was just a free-for-all, first come, first serve.

Although there hadn't been many other vehicles on the road, they had come across a few other people with the same idea, perhaps. Get home, lock the doors, and stay quiet. The other vehicles they came across hadn't been so lucky. In their rush, they had slid off the road and into ditches or other cars.

The only things that lit their path were the stars and moon above.

They passed one car whose horn was blaring with one long, drawn-out groan, the vehicle pressed in tight against an electrical pole. Although steam was still billowing out from the crumpled hood of the engine, the passengers were nowhere in sight.

Angela slammed on the brakes just long enough to take a sharp left onto Crocket Street toward her home, and then proceeded to regain speed.

"Slow down," Walter shouted, the noise of the car horn still blaring in the distance as they left it behind.

Angela didn't reply. And she definitely didn't slow down.

What she did do though, was stop. And without warning.

It was abrupt and deliberate.

The car screeched to a halt as the tires locked, sliding across the snow, and sending dirt and muddy snow water into the air. Walter fell forward in the back seat, his face almost making contact with the gear shifter mounted at the base of the center console.

Walter grunted hard as the car came to a stop. "What gives?"

"We're here," she said, running across the lawn of her front yard before Walter had a chance to even realize that she had taken the keys, unbuckled her belt, and slammed the driver's side door.

"I think we're here," old man Glen Moore said.

"What gave you that idea?" Walter laughed.

"You okay?" Glen started to unbuckle his seatbelt, and proceeded to climb out of the car.

"Yeah," Walter grumbled, climbing over the back of the front seat and out onto the snow covered lawn. "I'll live."

The snow crunched under the weight of his footfalls as the two men made their way up to Angela's house.

"Think she's all right?" Walter asked, listening to the crunch of each step as they walked.

"Hhhaa…." Old man Glen Moore laughed. "Don't you mean, *are we going to be all right*? This thing is happening to us, too. And with the power out, it's goin' to be gettin' very cold."

"True," Walter agreed as they made their way up the drive and into the front door that Angela had left open in her rush up the stairs.

Angela's house was small. But not nearly as small as what Walter could afford in North California on his meager minimum wage salary at the Dollar General. He was surprised to find that, unlike himself, her tastes and style choices had grown and matured.

Old man Glen Moore closed the front door as they entered the living room. Walter could hear a few people talking in another room, but found himself taking in the décor rather than listening to them. Aside from the fact that the living room floor looked like Hurricane Katrina had blown through, leaving a mess of toys and coloring books in its wake, the house was well-kept. The furniture was retro. The carpet, chairs, and even the coffee table all had hints of orange, red and brown. These fall colors accented the paintings that adorned the living room walls. Pictures of nature and family were interwoven along the walls, affixed in frames that matched the colors of the furniture and rug. The small flat screen TV that was mounted along one wall above an even smaller bookshelf had a crack running up the middle of it.

Walter stepped up to the bookshelf because he saw there were a few framed photos there. After closer inspection, his heart sank a little. He didn't know why he half expected to see a picture of himself standing by his Angela rather than this strange man that Walter didn't recognize. But he did.

"That's Lina's daddy," old man Glen Moore said, stepping up beside Walter by the TV.

"Yeah, I heard about it."

The two men stood there staring at the photo in the dark for a moment.

It was Walter who broke the silence.

"Hey…Glen," he said.

"Yeah…?"

"What did you mean back there in the pub kitchen? You know, that it was our fault that these giant crabs were happening. What did you mean by that? How in the world could any of this be our fault?"

"Well," Glen started.

Walter found it odd that he could see the old man's breath like a cloud of smoke as he breathed while they stood in Angela's living room. With his eyes adjusting to the darkness, he stared longingly into the old man's eyes and listened.

"It's our fault simply because *it is*, son," Glen said. "We've been fishin' those waters since the day of my father's father, if not longer."

"What does that have to do with anything?"

"Let me explain," he said, wrapping his arms around his chest to keep warm. "Every year we go out during crabbing season and catch close to eighty thousand pounds of king crab. We do this every year. At least, that is what we are told. This isn't the truth. Back in the early eighties, when I wasn't retired yet, we caught nearly a million pounds of crab every season. It's an impressive number, I know. Especially when you consider the numbers we are led to believe we are at now. Those numbers aren't true. I know because I live here. I see what comes in from those rigs every season. Last year we only brought in about ten thousand pounds of crab. When you look at those numbers, it just doesn't work. Not for a community that thrives off of the deep sea industry. We live and die by what these boys catch every season. And over the years the numbers have dropped exponentially."

"And…?"

"Well, think about it, boy." Old man Glen Moore shivered. "The community that thrives on this season can't thrive like it used to if the numbers are too low. In fact, if they get too low, the town will go under completely. That's just how this economy works, son. Always has. Always will."

"I'm sorry," Walter said, leading them into the kitchen because he quit hearing Angela's voice in the other room. "But, I'm still not really following you."

"Get it through your thick skull, boy." Glen Moore reached out and jabbed Walter in the chest with one wrinkly, liver-spotted finger. "What do you do when any food-related industry can't keep up with demand? What has any industry ever done? The cows are bigger and produce more milk. The chickens are bigger and lay more eggs. The pigs are so much bigger now that they finally get slaughtered after their legs can't even hold their own weight."

"What are you saying?" Walter asked. "You think that we've managed to introduce steroids into the crab supply out at sea? That's impossible. That's just completely ridiculous. This isn't one of your UFO stories, old man. You may not remember me, but you've been telling these kinds of stories since I was in middle school."

"I know who you are, Walter *Maninko*." Glen Moore put extra emphasis on the last name. "I knew your mother before you were even an idea. And you're right, this ain't one of them silly conspiracy ideas like all them others. You know how I know that?"

"How?"

"Because." Glen Moore stepped toward Walter, his teeth gritting with anger. "Because, I was on the board committee that passed the town vote to do that very thing. We did this. We introduced the growth hormones into their food supply. We've been doing it for the last five years. And last year we started to see some results. Although we didn't catch much in the sight of pounds, the amount we caught per crab was nearly double."

"They were growing?"

"You're damn right they was growing." Glen Moore backed away from Walter, a look of dread and disgust plastered across his face. "It's our fault. We made this happen. When we saw the growth this last season we got overzealous. Started introducing things into their diet that wasn't FDA regulated."

"Glen." Walter stepped forward to console him.

"No," Glen barked. "We should'a known better. We should'a done right. But we didn't. We had the right intentions, honestly. We was just looking out for the interest of the community. We didn't want our fishing jobs to go away. Without them, this town wouldn't thrive. My town wouldn't thrive. My home."

Old man Glen Moore sank into himself and began to cry.

"What's wrong?" Angela asked, stepping into the kitchen from the hallway.

Walter locked eyes with Glen, who was shaking his head. "Nothing," Walter said. "We'll talk about it later."

When he looked toward her he saw that she wasn't alone. Angela had a backpack slung over one shoulder. And from the looks of it, the bag was filled with supplies of some kind. To her right stood a girl that looked like she couldn't be Lina. She was too old. The girl was almost as tall as Angela, with dark black hair. And to Angela's left stood a little girl, probably around five or six years old. There was no mistaking it. This was her little girl. They both had that same long, fiery red hair that went down past their shoulders. All three women had the same terrified stare in their eyes.

"Maggie, this is Walter and Glen." Angela waved at them. "Boys, this is *Maggie*. She's been babysitting Lina while I work nights at the pub."

Both Walter and Glen smiled at the terrified teenager.

"Going somewhere?" Walter asked, nodding toward the backpack.

"Yeah," Angela said, leaning down slightly and grabbing her daughter by the hand. "Somewhere warm."

"A'men to that," old man Glen Moore agreed, still slightly shivering, his breath visible even in the darkness of the unlit kitchen.

"What do you have in mind?" Walter asked.

"The police station," she said. "I dated a guy that works there. He told me they have backup generators in case the town backups don't come on. This way they can still respond to calls in an emergency."

Walter laughed to himself. "Let me guess. The sheriff?"

"What?"

"The sheriff," Walter said again. "You dated the sheriff?"

"No," she scoffed. "He was the deputy, thank you very much."

Albeit brief, they shared a passing smile at one another.

"That sounds like a plan to me," Maggie said, pulling her long, dark hair out of her face. "This place is getting colder the longer we stand here."

"Then what are we waitin' for?" Glen said. "Let's get before we ain't got the opportunity to."

"What about my parents?" Maggie said.

"Chances are, your parents had the same idea," Angela assured. "And if not, I'm sure Deputy Chandler will get you to them as soon as we get there."

"Okay," she said with a sigh.

"I don't know about you, but I am done standing around." Glen Moore rubbed his shivering hands together.

And with that, they were out the front door and back toward the cramped space of Angela's Honda Civic.

Chapter 10

Walter, Angela, Lina, Maggie and old man Glen Moore all made it to the police station without incident. That isn't to suggest, however, that they didn't see a few horrific things along the way.

A few blocks before making it to the station, they watched in horror as a fire truck careened down the road at an alarming rate, its red and white sirens flashing their brilliant hue. The flashing lights lit up the cold November night as the onlookers inside the Honda Civic watched with dismay. Just before the giant crab that had been riding on the top of the fire truck was thrown off by the crash, its massive pincer pierced the driver's side window, reaching inside. Even over the sound of the roaring fire truck siren, they heard the cries of the driver as he was pulled from the truck. It was then that the truck tilted, tipping into a parked truck before flipping three times into the snow. The giant crab toppled with it, being crushed beneath the weight of the large fire truck.

But that wasn't all they saw.

They even passed one house on an unlit suburban block that had its lights on. That particular house must have had a generator, because they were the only house with power. As if the lights in the home were a beacon of unrest to the giant crabs and their smaller companions, the house was under siege as the Honda Civic drove by. Luckily, all of the monsters tearing their way through the home were too preoccupied to take notice of the passengers in the small car as it kept on going.

Walter had almost assumed that the police station would be not much better a place to hide than anywhere else. It seemed like the giant monster crabs had done a number on most of the town already. He didn't think there would really be anywhere safe to hide from these ravenous creatures.

But to his surprise, when they arrived at the police station, the parking lot was void of activity. There were no lights on either, which wasn't much of a good sign considering the reason they made the trip.

"What do you want to do?" Walter asked from the backseat, with Lina sitting in his lap and Maggie cramped at his side.

They all looked through the Honda Civic windshield toward the empty police station parking lot and beyond.

"I don't know," Angela said.

"Think anyone's in there?" Glen asked.

"Only one way to find out." Walter reached over the seat, grabbing Angela on the shoulder. "Let's go knock on the door."

"I guess you're right," Angela agreed. She put the car back into drive and slowly eased the vehicle toward the front door. Once she got close enough, she put it into park and yanked the key out of the ignition. "You guys ready?"

Walter caught her gaze in the rearview mirror and nodded. When he looked over to Glen, he saw that the old man was nodding, as well.

Angela reached her hand out to the door handle, and before she could pull it and step out into the cold, a massive explosion erupted in the distance, several miles to the east. The night sky lit up in a momentary eclipse of bright brilliance. And just like that, the light was gone.

"What the hell was that?" Maggie asked, all of them craning their necks toward the sudden burst of light and sound.

"My guess," old man Glen Moore said as they watched what appeared to be a steady fire in the distance, the light of the fire altering the darkness on that side of town. "I'd say it was the old Dine and Pump. Gas station pumps must'a went up."

"I'm scared," Lina mumbled, trying to reach for her mommy.

"I'm scared, too," Walter assured her with a soothing voice, and then looked up at Angela in the rearview mirror. "I don't know about you, but now seems like as a good a time as any to check that front door."

She nodded, proceeding to step out of the car. "If we're getting out, everyone is."

With that, Glen unbuckled his seatbelt and opened the door.

*****

"No, I'm afraid you're the only people that've tried their luck at comin' to the station," Dotty said, a plume of cigarette smoke billowing around her face, the cigarette in her hand already almost down to the filter. "Don't blame you one bit for headin' this way, either. I'd'a done the same thing, too, if I'd lost power at my place."

"But what about the power here?" Walter asked, looking around the unlit lobby.

"It'll be on soon enough. Just give it time," Dotty said, taking a long, hard drag from her cigarette. "The generators in the basement need to warm up before the juice kicks on. I was just down there. So, hopefully the backup power'll be on in another couple of minutes or so."

"Do you really think so?"

"Of course, I think so." She glared at Walter. "Who do you think I am, young man? A liar?"

"I didn't mean it like that," he said. "It's just that…."

"It's just that we're all a little shaken up." Angela stepped forward. "Is anyone else here besides yourself?"

"Oh, yes," Dotty said. "Sheriff Mathew and the deputy are here. Unfortunately, that's everyone. Before the power went out, the lines were blowing up with calls, and all of our on-duty officers got sent out. We haven't heard back from any of 'em."

Walter thought to tell her what they had seen happen to the firetruck, but decided best not to. He didn't want to add any undue tension to the already overwhelmingly tense situation.

Instead, he said, "Well, if you have two officers that are here, where are they?"

"They're in the back." Dotty stamped out her cigarette in the ashtray at her desk and pointed. "I'll take you all to see them."

Walter, Angela, Lina, Maggie and Glen all followed toe-to-heel as the chain-smoking office receptionist led the way through the dark police station lobby, and beyond a narrow hallway of offices and interrogation rooms that never got used. Once past this part of the station, Walter and the others found themselves standing in the doorway of what looked to be a break room. In the center of the table in this room were two flashlights turned on and facing upward. It was in this dimly-lit room amidst the refrigerator, coffee pot, and microwave that the two officers were found combing through a stack of ammunition.

"Broomberg...Chandler...." Dotty cleared her throat. "We've got visitors."

The two officers looked away from the task they were engrossed in with unexpected glimmers in their eyes.

"Angela." The tall, skinny officer stood from the break room table, setting the ammunition he had in hand down. "Thank God you're okay."

"Bart," Angela said, accepting his embrace.

Walter watched this act with disdain.

When the hug ended, Deputy Bart Chandler said, "And Lina?"

"She's right here," Angela said, stepping away from the doorway to show that she wasn't alone.

"Good," Bart said. "Who are your other friends? Well, besides Glen. Everybody already knows that old fart."

"This is Maggie, my babysitter. And this is Walter. We went to school together a long time ago."

We went to school together, Walter thought. *More like we were in love. Big difference.*

And before he could let it show on his face, Walter reminded himself that it, in fact, had been a very long time ago. Just because he still felt the same way didn't mean she would. And he had no right to assume that things could ever be the way they used to be back then.

"Walter Maninko." Walter stepped forward, extending his right hand.

Bart shook Walter's hand and nodded. "Deputy Chandler. But you can call me Bart."

"We came here hoping you had power. The plan is to just lay low until things are under control. But we'd rather not freeze to death before that happens. No such luck?"

"Oh, we'll have power. Don't you worry about that." Sheriff Broomberg stepped up to the group, wiping a small handgun with a rag. "Just give it a few more minutes. Generators tend to take a while to warm up this time a year. We kind'a had the same idea."

"How so?"

"Well, I don't know if you can tell or not," Sheriff Broomberg grumbled, "but this situation is just a little bit out of our control. A little bit above pay grade, if you will. So, the plan is much like the one you had."

"And that is…?"

"To wait." the Sheriff quit wiping the gun with the rag and locked eyes with Walter. "To wait until the power gets turned back on and get someone on the phone that can handle this mess. There's no telling how many of our officers we've lost tonight, and I don't even want to start thinkin' about it."

Refusing to look away from this short man's attempt at an intimidation tactic, Walter kept eye-contact. "I'm sorry to hear that. What can we do to help?"

"I like you already, boy." The sheriff patted Walter on the arm. "Ever shot a gun before?"

"I have, but it's been a few years."

"How long is a few?" Bart chimed in.

Walter laughed. "Oh, I don't know…like fifteen. Last time I shot a gun was when I lived here, actually."

"Well, then." Sheriff Broomberg took Walter's right hand, forcing it palm up, and dropped the handgun into it. "Looks like you're our man."

"What do mean?" Walter inspected the gun.

"So far we've been lucky and the station hasn't seen any activity. However, that might change. Once the power kicks on, I plan to get on the horn with the higher-ups. See if we can't get some air support in here to clean this mess up. Assess the damage. But even still. Once that call gets made, it ain't goin' to happen right then and there. We'll still have to hold up until help arrives."

"How long will that be?" Glen Moore asked.

"I don't know, old man." Sheriff Broomberg cleared his throat. "I really don't know."

The room fell silent for a few moments.

"And that's why you have just been officially deputized," the sheriff said, patting Walter on the shoulder.

"Seriously?"

"Seriously," Bart insisted. "If those things decide to try to get in here while we're waiting for help to come, we need all the help we can get. And unless some more people decide to leave their homes to come this way, looks like you guys are it."

Walter nodded, studying the weight of the handgun as he balanced it in both palms.

"But do you really think it's going to—?"

Walter's words were cut short by a sudden *click* and the steady hum that rattled up toward the break room from the police station basement.

The overhead lights in the break room flickered to life.

They had power.

"Thank you, Jesus." Glen Moore rubbed his cold hands together. "Someone point me to the heater."

"I can feel it shaking the floor." Lina giggled.

"That means we're in business, sweetheart." Bart knelt and gave the little girl a high five.

Everything was going to be okay.

Chapter 11

Most of the town was in utter turmoil and chaos of devastating horrors. The bloodbath that engulfed the citizens of Seward, Alaska, seemed to have no end. With the rise of these giant monsters from the depths of the sea, they had begun to devour any living thing that crossed their paths. Humans, cats, dogs, and even squirrels and rats alike all eventually succumbed to the same grueling, visceral end.

The streets were filled with the carnage of these gorging creatures and the scraps of their feasting that was left in their wake.

At first, these creatures were busy devouring anything that they came across. But after a while that became scarce. The food source was in hiding. Many of the creatures got lucky, finding their way into the local grocery store where much of the tender human flesh was ripe for the taking. They managed to make their way into the store without any effort. All they had to do was walk up and the double doors slid away all by themselves. Access to the quivering and running meat was plentiful. But even so, this food source dissipated.

With the screams fading in the store and in the streets, the creatures began tearing the city apart. It was no different than burrowing in the sands of the ocean floor. There was bound to be food somewhere.

And their instincts had been correct.

People had been hiding in their homes. Their cars. Their trailers. And their sheds.

As the night went on and the slaughter ensued, it was becoming harder and harder to find sustenance. The creatures resorted to what they did best. Wait and listen. The vibrations in the ocean floor told them when something was near. Either predator or prey.

And the same could be said here on land, as well.

They waited and they listened.

Occasionally the vibrations would start up, leading the giant sea monsters to the thing they desired. Other times it led them to large predators that either electrocuted them or blew them up in big balls of gas-filled fire.

But now, the vibration that they heard was coming from somewhere else. Somewhere new. Somewhere recent.

With their attentions now drawn to the subtle inclinations of a potential feeding, the crabs, both big and small, made their move.

It would be no time at all before they fell upon that vibration source with ravenous delight.

As far as the east was from the west on the coastlines of Seward, Alaska, the thrumming clatter of countless crab steps seemed to have no end. They were all headed in the same direction.

Toward that very thing that so eagerly tantalized the long antenna set on either side of each compound eye.

The crabs were on the move.

Chapter 12

"Well, what did they say?"

"Honestly, I don't think he believed me." Sheriff Mathew Broomberg set the phone back down onto the receiver.

Walter sighed.

Everyone had been standing there listening in on the one-sided conversation as the sheriff relayed the happenings of the disaster to the county dispatch disaster unit two towns over on the other side of the mountains.

As the sheriff had stood there pacing back and forth with the phone pressed to his ear, everyone watched with anticipation. Walter was sitting at one of the chairs in the lobby next to Lina, who happened to be coloring in one of the lobby magazines with some markers that her mother had brought with her in her backpack. Old man Glen Moore was slouched against the receptionist desk with both elbows propped up on it for support. He looked tired and worn down. Angela was standing with Bart only a few feet away from the pacing sheriff. Dotty was smoking another cigarette, still within earshot of the sheriff's conversation. She was standing away from everyone else, near the glass front double doors leading into the dark police station parking lot. Maggie stood with them, nestled under one arm of the tall deputy. She seemed most terrified out of everyone in the room.

Walter wasn't actually sure how he felt yet. It was all just happening so fast it seemed like he didn't really have much time to react to any of it. He felt like he was floating in a bad dream and that nothing he could do would change the outcome of the nightmare. All he wanted more than anything was to wake up. But he knew he wasn't going to. The handgun resting in his front pocket was too heavy to seem like it was all just a dream, no matter how bad he wanted it to be.

"What do you mean, *he didn't believe you*?" old man Glen Moore asked, stepping away from the receptionist desk.

"I mean...." Sheriff Broomberg gritted his teeth while jabbing his open hand toward the phone. "The mouth breather thought I was pullin' his leg. He mostly just laughed at me the whole time."

"What are we going to do?" Angela asked.

"I'm scared," Maggie said, pressing herself even tighter into the deputy's chest.

"Is there someone else we can call?" Walter asked from the lobby seating area.

"Let me think," the sheriff said with sarcasm. "Let me go to the pisser real quick and shit out a few numbers for you."

"I understand you're stressed here, Sheriff." Deputy Bart Chandler stepped away from Maggie and toward his commanding officer. "But that type of attitude isn't going to solve anything. So what if the CDDU didn't take your seriously? Call them again. And again...and again, until they send someone. And when we've done that, let's call the FBI. The CIA. The president, for crying out loud. We need to get ahold of somebody, don't we?"

"Yeah." Sheriff Broomberg laughed.

"Do I look like I'm joking, Sheriff?" The deputy scooped up the phone and shoved it into his boss's hand. "Now, make that call. And call again. We need help. Anyone's help."

Bart stormed off, heading toward the back of the police station.

Angela went after him, leaving Maggie standing there all alone.

"Somebody'll come," Dotty said, puffing on her cancer stick, all the while not taking her eyes off the parking lot outside.

"I hope you're right," old man Glen Moore said. "I hope you're right."

Walter sighed, watching Lina color all over the magazine in her lap. He was amazed at how much she looked like Angela now that he was able to get a good look at her with the power back on. Her hair was fiery red and her skin was that same milky complexion as her mother's. He looked up, noticing that Maggie was standing alone. Beyond her, the sheriff was on the phone, now talking with someone else. This time he didn't seem as tense or distressed. Hopefully, that was a good sign.

Standing to his feet and stepping away from Lina, Walter nodded toward Dotty, and then toward the little girl. Dotty nodded back as if understanding that she should watch her. Feeling confident that they were on the same page, he stepped up to the old man.

"Ben, right?"

"No," he said, no longer shaking now that the building had warmed back up. "It's Glen…Glen Moore."

"Right, I'm sorry." Walter put one hand on his shoulder. "Been a little preoccupied with what's been happening."

"No hard feelings." Glen smiled.

"Hey." Walter leaned in and started to whisper. "Think you can do me a solid and keep an eye of these three ladies? I'm going to go see what's going on with Angela and that other policeman."

"Sure thing," Glen said.

"Maybe you can help get Maggie to think of something else," Walter continued. "She seems freaked out the most by all of this. Maybe see if Angela brought a game or something in that bag of hers."

"I can do that." Glen nodded.

"Okay, great." Walter started to walk away.

"And, Walter," the old man called out. "His name is, Bart…Deputy Bart Chandler."

"Thanks." Walter waved, not stopping as he passed by the sheriff, who appeared to be jotting down something onto a notepad with the phone still pressed to one ear.

Hopefully that was a good thing.

Hopefully someone was coming to help them.

And soon.

Walter met up with Angela and Bart in an office. The name on the door read *Sheriff Broomberg*. Both of them were riffling through papers strewn across the desks and digging through filing cabinets along one wall that were stuffed with papers.

"What are you guys looking for?" Walter asked, stepping into the office.

"Numbers to anyone that can help us. FEMA, the Alaskan Coast Guard, you name it," Bart said, not looking up as he skimmed a sheet of paper.

"Can I help?" Walter asked.

"Sure," the deputy said, grabbing a stack of papers off the desk and handing them to Walter. "Start looking through these."

Before Walter could take the papers into his hand, Dotty darted into the room, heaving with shortness of breath.

Coughing, she said, "We've got company."

"What?"

"They're here," she said. "They're in the streets cutting across the barbershop and into the parking lot as we speak."

And as if to help insinuate the distress in her voice, a loud crash of what sounded like breaking glass, followed by a sudden scream, reverberated down the hall from the police station lobby.

A gunshot rang out, causing Angela to scream.

"Lina!"

Chapter 13

You would think with the situation as it was unfolding, it would be something to run away from. But that wasn't what Walter Maninko was doing at all. In fact, he was doing the opposite. There was a part of him that knew he was no hero. That he was just a loser that managed a Dollar General and got paid minimum wage. He was far from anyone's hero. The true reason he knew this to be fact was the idea that he was merely chasing after Angela as she rushed toward the lobby to instinctively protect her child. Had she not been there leading him toward the danger, he would have done what he usually did in any time of crisis: hide or pretend it wasn't happening until it went away.

But this wasn't something that was going to go away.

He followed Bart and Angela. He followed the screams. The sounds of gunfire. And the sounds of those things slamming their massive pincers. His heart pounded in his chest with each thrumming charge forward as his heels pounded into the floor with each rushing step.

He tried to keep up, and the handgun in his front pocket bounced up and down, reminding him that he even had it.

"Lina!" Angela shouted.

Guns were going off. The explosive report as each gun was fired echoed in the small space of the lobby.

CLICK...CLICK...CLICK...

A cold breeze blew into the room from the two busted glass front doors.

The screams were making it hard for Walter to think straight. When he stopped running, it wasn't because he had gotten close enough to the rest of his group to begin firing his weapon. He quit running because he got a look at what was happening.

Three smaller crabs rushed into the busted doorway, darting across broken glass. There was a giant crab behind them trying to force its way in through the doorway. It wouldn't be long before it was in the lobby with them just like that one eventually got into the pub.

Sheriff Broomberg fired at the creatures as they charged forward. His gun jerked in his hand with each pull of the trigger. His aim was precise and with intention. Each time that the gun shook in his hand, Walter watched as one of those things took a direct hit. The smaller creatures only took one or two shots before falling where they stood, motionless. But, for every one that fell to the lobby floor dead, another came skittering through the open doorway from outside. Broomberg kept on firing.

"Get behind me," Bart shouted, directing Angela to get out of the way.

Angela darted past him back toward Walter, with Lina in her arms.

With his pistol in hand, Bart began to unload his weapon on the mass of crabs as they tried to gain ground.

Two more went down as their exoskeletons erupted into meaty chunks.

The giant crab at the door was suddenly met with another also trying to make its way in.

CLICK...CLICK...CLICK...

A giant pincer sliced at the air from outside, trying desperately to get in.

"Oh, god," Angela shouted. "Someone's got to help them."

That was when Walter finally stumbled out of his daze and into the situation.

Help them, he thought, looking around the lobby from his safe position behind Bart, who was still firing his weapon into the creatures.

That was when he realized that something was wrong.

Old man Glen Moore and Angela's babysitter, Maggie, were hunched down behind a plastic potted tree in one corner of the lobby next to the double doors. If they stepped out and tried to run for it, they would either be grabbed by the giant red pincer swinging back and forth in the open doorway, or would be gunned down by the barrage of gunfire that Bart and Mathew were unleashing on the creatures.

"What do we do?" Angela shouted.

"I don't know," Walter said, finally taking the gun from his front pocket into his hand.

He took aim and readied for the recoil, tightening his grip. He wasn't sure how bad the gun was going to jerk when he pulled the trigger.

"We could use a little help," Sheriff Broomberg shouted, looking toward Walter as he stopped to reload his weapon.

Walter pulled the trigger.

Nothing happened.

CLICK…CLICK…CLICK…

The lobby floor was littered with more than two dozen smaller, gunned down crabs. But that didn't matter, because more were coming in every second.

"The safety," Bart shouted over his shoulder.

Walter frantically looked at the side of the gun, releasing the safety.

He aimed and pulled the trigger. The gun rocked in his hand so hard that he almost dropped it. Even still, his shot had counted. One of those things took a direct hit right in the abdomen as it leapt up to attack. As soon as it fell, another one charged in from outside to take its place.

"We're going to run out of ammo," Walter shouted, pulling the trigger, this time prepared for the gun's recoil.

A crab took the bullet in the right pincer, spinning in place as its right arm erupted in a meaty gush of gore. Walter fired again, the second shot sending it to the ground, never to get up again.

"You think I don't know that?" Bart said, shouting between each squeeze.

The Seward police station lobby was a volley of noise. If there were any crabs that didn't know of their whereabouts before this, one thing was certain. Their place was made known now. The gunfire had to be echoing through the cold, moonlit night across the mountains and back again.

Walter fired into the open doorway three more times before his gun finally *clicked* empty. "What do I do, what do I do?"

"Here, take mine!" Bart tossed him his gun and quickly exchanged them while slamming a new magazine into the one he had just received. He was back to firing his weapon before Walter. But Walter wasn't far behind.

Walter squeezed the trigger. His hands were burning. The gun felt hot in his grip.

"Help me," Maggie shouted from the corner of the lobby, a giant crab arm swaying wildly out in front of her.

Glen was behind her holding her tightly. Keeping her from rushing out and into the danger.

"Do something!" Dotty and Angela shouted together.

"Cover me." Sheriff Broomberg dropped his handgun and pulled up a shotgun. "We need to get them out'a there."

When the shotgun went off, it was like a bellowing cannon of dynamite.

Walter's ears rang.

The shotgun went off again, and this time Sheriff Broomberg was stepping out from behind the desk and into the lobby.

"Cover him," Deputy Bart Chandler shouted. "Focus your shots on the big ones in the doorway. I'm a better shot. Let me take care of the little ones as they come in."

Walter wasn't sure how he even managed to hear any of that with his ears ringing like they were. But he did. And as the deputy had asked, he did. He pulled his gun away from the base of the doorway, where those things had been entering, and aimed at the two giant monsters still trying to press their way into the small opening.

He fired, watching as red outer skeleton and meaty chunks erupted in the large pincer of the creature closest to Glen and the girl. With his agenda figured out, Walter just kept on firing. As he fired, the gun burning his palms with its violent jolt, he watched as the sheriff reached out for Maggie.

He fired again, this time hitting his target a little too high. The bullet grazed the creature, piercing the wall beyond it.

Focus, Walter thought, aiming again.

CLICK…CLICK…

Just as he started to pull the trigger again, he heard Bart shout, "There's too many."

With his focus no longer on the giant pincer in the doorway, Walter realized that they were going get overrun.

The scream of pain that came next was what made Walter realize he had quit firing his weapon.

But the scream didn't last long. The shout had been sharp and high-pitched, then abruptly ended, giving way to the sound of gurgling groans. As Sheriff Mathew Broomberg had tried to pull Maggie to safety, the giant pincer jutting into the lobby from outside clamped shut around his waist. Blood spewed from the sheriff's mouth and eyes. Maggie screamed in terror. Gunfire boomed. Creatures fell, the lobby full of crab bodies now.

"Move." Old man Glen Moore shoved Maggie forward. If they were going to make it through, now was the time while the giant thing was preoccupied with the sheriff.

Maggie didn't seem to want to budge. She just stood there, screaming. When the giant pincer wrapped around Sheriff Broomberg's waist let go, the police officer fell into two halves onto the police station lobby floor. All of the smaller crabs that were rushing into the lobby were now preoccupied with his corpse. Blood spilled out from his body, his intestines strewn across the blood-soaked carpet as the frenzied creatures began their feast.

The monsters were hungry.

The sensation of food at their feet excited not only them, but the giant crabs still stuck outside. They became violent. Shoving harder against the opening. Swinging their pincers harder and faster, desperate to get inside before all the food was gone.

"Go," Angela shouted, waving Glen and Maggie to run to safety.

Glen shoved her forward, encouraging her to run. To jump over the feasting horde of crabs and never stop moving.

CLICK…CLICK…CLICK…

But that wasn't what happened at all.

When Glen shoved Maggie, she screamed, slipping in the bloody gore of Sheriff Mathew Broomberg's scattered entrails. Falling forward, she tried to catch herself, but failed to do so. Glen shouted out, trying to catch her. Bart fired on the creatures feasting on his boss's corpse. Angela held her daughter tightly from safety behind Walter and Bart. Bart kept firing.

Walter just stood there with his gun raised, eyes wide, mind melting with disbelief. As if in some type of frozen capsule of the mind's distant memory, he watched in horrific slow motion as the two giant crabs trying to get in finally seemed to press hard enough that part of the doorway gave. Particle board, drywall and dust fell as the opening became wider. With the newly-acquired space, the creature Walter had been firing upon reached in, deeper this time, into the lobby, catching Maggie by the leg as she fell.

She screamed out in pain.

Crimson splashed from her thigh as her knee and everything below it fell to the floor to join the meal being enjoyed by the smaller horde of crabs at her feet.

The second that her screaming, shaking body fell to the floor, it was covered by four gnashing crabs as they surrounded her, tearing her apart alive.

The framing around the doorway gave in even more with a loud, grumbling wooden groan. And with that, the first giant crab stepped into the lobby, joining in on the feast.

"We've got to move," Walter shouted, grabbing Bart by the arm.

CLICK...CLICK...CLICK...

"We can't leave Glen," Dotty shouted.

"We have no choice," Deputy Chandler demanded, grabbing Angela by the shirt and pulling her along. "Let's go."

"Where are you taking us?" Walter shouted, giving chase as Bart led them all down the narrow hall and away from the slaughter that was taking place in the lobby.

"We've got to get someplace safe while their focus is on something other than us!"

Walter looked back and saw that there were now two giant crabs in the lobby, along with more than a dozen smaller crabs. They were all busy slopping up bits of gore, blood and viscera. Old man Glen Moore was still standing in the corner of the lobby, huddled down behind the fake tree with an expression or terror glued to his face.

"What's the plan?" Walter said, turning away from the horrific scene and focusing on the people that were still alive. "Where are we going?"

"The basement," Deputy Bart said, very matter-of-fact. "We've got more weapons down there. If they do break in, the narrow staircase will make it harder for the larger ones to get in, and we can pick them off." As he opened the door leading to the basement, he shoved his gun into Walter's hands. "And if they break through that, we can always access the outside through one of the basement panel windows."

The first person to start her way down into the basement was Angela, Lina still held tightly in her arms. Next followed Dotty, who looked so pale, Walter thought she might faint. After Walter stepped in, Bart followed behind, slamming the door shut.

"Help me barricade this door!"

Chapter 14

"Glen is dead. We left him out there." Dotty shook with panic as she tried to light a cigarette. She couldn't keep her hands still long enough to get the lighter to strike. "We left him out there. Glen is dead because we left him."

"We had to," Angela screamed, stilling holding Lina in her arms a little too tightly.

"You're hurting me, Momma."

"I'm sorry, baby." Angela set her daughter down. "Just stay close."

"We killed him."

"Would you shut up?" Bart argued. "We had to. There was no way to get to him."

"I'll shut the hell up as soon as I get this damn thing lit."

Walter stepped over to the old woman, taking the lighter. "Here," he said, and with one flick of the thumb, the lighter worked.

Dotty leaned in, touching the tip of her shaking cigarette to the flame. After a few puffs she was satisfied, accepting the lighter back.

"We have to come up with a plan," Walter said. "We can't stay down here forever."

The sound of feasting was still very apparent even downstairs in the basement. As long as they were quiet, they could hear the clattering of many feet rummaging about above them, most likely still gobbling up the bits of what was left of their friends.

The Seward Police Station basement was damp and poorly lit, but rather spacious. It spanned the entire width and length of the station above. The narrow doorway that opened up to the staircase leading downstairs was currently being barricaded with a small refrigerator that Bart said used to be in the break room upstairs, back when it used to still work. Other than that, the door was locked, and it helped that it opened out into the station rather than in toward the basement. If those things got in, at least they would hear it first when the small fridge decided to topple down the staircase.

At the base of those stairs was a set of light switches. Four switches in total. Two of them kept the basement lights on when flicked in the right position. One of the switches was somehow rigged to the small generator at the far corner of the room. The switch was currently *on*, the generator lightly throbbing with life. Without the power, everything would go out again and things would start to get cold.

Although Walter didn't think Dotty had heard Bart in her rambling panic, the deputy had assured them that the emissions from the generator were properly ventilated and that they wouldn't suffocate on gas fumes or anything like that. As reassuring as the cop was trying to be, asphyxiation seemed like a much better way to go than getting torn into bits by ravenous overgrown crabs.

Between the generators, along the same wall as the light switches, were a row of narrow windows that looked out into the back parking lot, which was fenced-in. This fenced area housed parked police cars and a few golf carts fitted with snow tires. Although the windows were thin, it was nice to know that ground level was within reach if things got ugly. Just bust the window and start pushing people through it. From what he could tell, looking out into this fenced parking lot with only the moonlight to see, it seemed like there were no crabs in sight. It didn't matter how that made him feel, because Walter was sure that nothing short of death was going to ever keep his heart from pounding this hard ever again.

Aside from this, there was a caged-in area with a keypad-style lock on it that made up most of the basement floor. Inside this caged-in area were tons of empty shelves. It looked like this was more than likely the evidence locker, but since nothing ever happened in Seward, the shelves probably stayed empty. Most of the overhead lighting that covered this section of the basement was turned off, leaving the rest of the grimy room dim and desolate.

"That's it," Dotty spat. "I'm dead. I'm goin'a die. That's all there is to it. Sixty years of chain smoking and giant sea monsters are what finally did me in. I just can't believe it. I'm dead… dead… dead…."

"Would you give it a rest?" Bart said. "No one else is going to die. Okay?"

"And what makes you so sure, Deputy?"

"Just smoke your cigarettes and keep the comments to yourself, please."

"Yeah," Angela agreed. "You're scaring Lina."

Dotty stared at Lina for a while, her face at first hard and distance, but eventually breaking down and becoming subdued. "I'm sorry," she said. "I'm just scared, is all."

"We all are," Walter said, stepping under a light, shadows dancing across the left side of his face and chest as he swayed. "But we need to stay calm. The Sheriff made a few calls. Surely he got through to someone. Help is on the way. All we need to do is keep quiet and stay level-headed. Everything will be okay if we can manage to do those two things."

Bart nodded in agreement.

Overhead, something shifted hard. Their faint CLICKS could be heard through the walls. The sound was muffled, but still very present.

Something slammed against the basement door.

The refrigerator rocked in place, but didn't topple down the stairs. The door boomed again.

They were on the other side now, trying to get in.

Lina began to whimper.

"It'll hold," Bart insisted.

Without even thinking about it, as if Lina were his own child, Walter scooped the terrified child up into his arms and held her close. Rocking her as he bounced on his heels, he whispered to her that he wouldn't let anything happen.

"You promise?" She winced, another thundering boom shocking the basement door above them.

"I promise," he said, kissing her on the forehead. "Everything is going to be okay."

"They're goin'a get in and eat us all," Dotty shouted, throwing her half-smoked cigarette toward the staircase.

Angela stepped up and slapped the old woman hard across the face. The sound of meat against meat as her cheek glistened red echoed across the basement floor over the sounds of stomping and thrashing overhead. Whatever those things were doing up there, it was safe to assume they were tearing the place apart. It sounded as if the tables, chairs, desks, and doors were getting beaten to death as those things upped their forage for more.

"I...am so...sorry." Angela pulled back, realizing she had just struck the old woman.

"I'm fine," Dotty said, dismayed, holding one hand to her cheek. "I just need a cigarette."

The old woman started digging in her pockets for another.

The basement door slammed again, this time shaking the small refrigerator good enough that it almost toppled over that time. Everyone's eyes were fixed on the refrigerator as it came to rest back in its place atop the staircase.

As it settled, Dotty began to pace. "I'm out of cigarettes. I am out of mother—"

"Woman, I do not want to have to tell you again." Walter stepped toward her, grabbing her by the shirt while still holding Lina in his other arm. "You are causing a ruckus, and it is scaring Lina. Now, if you please. Go over there." He shoved her. "Sit down. And do us all a favor and shut up. Do you *got that*?"

"Now you listen here." Dotty grabbed him back. "I was swingin' punches before you was even born. Who the hell do you think you are tellin' me what to do anyhow? You abandoned this town when it needed you all those years ago and you're goin'a abandon us just the same as soon as the opportunity seems right."

"That's not true," Walter shouted over the *whooping* sound outside.

"Everybody, shut up," Deputy Bart demanded.

"You don't know who I am or what I've done," Walter continued anyway. "Who the hell are you to judge me for leaving back then? You don't know why I left."

"Ha!" Dotty laughed, egging him on.

"Would you two shut up and listen," Bart shouted, to no avail.

"I know what I missed out on when I left. You hear me?" Walter jammed his finger in Dotty's face. "And I don't need a wrinkled old hag like you reminding me. You got that? I could have had her forever. We could have been in love always. Lina could be my little girl. But she's not. I realize that. I realize I threw it all away when I left here. And for what, a stupid minimum wage job at the Dollar General? I made a mistake, okay? I should have never—"

"For the last time." Bart stepped up, butting himself between Dotty and Walter. "Would you shut up and listen?"

"What?" Walter barked, realizing he hadn't meant to shout in the officer's face.

"Just listen," Bart said quietly, his eyes to the ceiling.

At first, all that Walter could hear was the stomping and banging that was going on inside the station above them. But then, after a moment, he heard it. The *whooping* sound coming from outside.

It sounded like a helicopter.

"We're saved," Angela said, pointing toward the narrow windows along the wall.

Outside, everyone watched with surprise as a set of lights beamed down from above onto the back fenced parking lot of the police station. It was a helicopter. No question.

"Yes," Walter said, wrapping an arm around Angela and kissing Lina on the forehead again.

Walter was so excited to see the light as it danced across the parking lot that he didn't even realize that Angela was leaning into him, kissing him on the cheek.

They were actually going to be okay.

"How are they going to know we're down here?" Dotty asked.

"We need to signal them somehow," Lina said, sounding like a full-blown adult.

"You're right," Bart said. "We've got to get out there before they fly—"

His words were cut short by a startling sound as the refrigerator toppled down the stairs toward them. The basement door burst open, splintering into bits, as one giant pincer jutted through the opening.

Dotty was the first one to scream.

Chapter 15

"How do I get one of these windows open?" Walter shouted, half a dozen small crabs rushing down the basement steps toward them.

Deputy Bart Chandler pulled his pistol and fired it once. One of the narrow windows to Walter's right shattered in succession with the deafening blast. Without feeling the need to ask any further questions, Walter rushed toward the broken window, and proceeded to break it even more with his elbow. As he did this, he watched Bart turn toward the staircase, firing his weapon.

CLICK...CLICK...

"Lina first," Walter said, helping the little girl up to the window. He watched as several small crabs burst into bits, Bart's precision the only thing keeping them alive. "You're almost there."

With Lina through the opening, now standing in the fenced back parking lot of the police station, he waved for Angela to go. As he started to help her, two small crabs got beyond the barrier Bart had been providing with his pistol.

"Had to reload," Bart shouted, jamming a fresh magazine into place before taking aim once more.

Dotty screamed.

One of the crabs that had gotten past Bart leapt into the air, landing on the old woman. She fell back, stumbling to the ground as the thing writhed and snipped with its two pincers.

Walter kicked one clear across the room, its shell shattering as it hit the wall beside a generator. Satisfied, he turned to Dotty, who was still being attacked. He kicked hard, sending the thing off of her.

She screamed again, her bloodied arms covering the scratches, and with swollen marks on her face. Before helping her to her feet, Walter stomped out the creature, its muscles and meat spreading out across the basement floor. When he lifted her up, she was covered in blood. That thing's pincers had done a number on her arms and face. It looked like part of her left ear was missing. Rather than ask her if she was okay, he looked to the window. Angela was gone.

"Go," he said, pushing Dotty toward the window. "I'm right behind you."

Pulling out his gun, Walter stepped next to Bart, looking up the staircase. The doorway was too narrow for the massive creature. Its huge pincer thrashed about wildly.

"It won't get in," Bart shouted, pulling this trigger, sending one of those things off the staircase to its doom. "That part of the doorframe is encased with cement. No way that thing'll get through."

Walter started to fire. He squeezed the trigger twice. The first shot missed and the second shot took off a leg. But that didn't stop the crab. It kept coming. Bart fired at the crab Walter had missed, sending it down for good.

"We need to go," Walter shouted, looking back toward the window. "The girls are already outside."

"I'll hold them off," Deputy Bart shouted.

CLICK...CLICK...CLICK...

"What are you talking about, man? We don't need a hero. Come on."

Bart laughed, firing his pistol into the mob as they came down the staircase one by one. "I don't plan on it. Go ahead and get through the window. Once you're out, duck down and cover me from there so I can make it."

"Got it," Walter shouted back. He fired one more shot into the mob before turning toward the window.

As he ran toward it, he saw three sets of shoes standing nearby, beside one of the cars. He could still hear the whooping sound of the helicopter overhead. Even though he couldn't see their beaming lights, at least the sound made him know that it was still close by. He tossed the gun out into the parking lot and proceeded to climb through. It wasn't as easy as Lina had made it look, but he was getting by. With a few tugs and grunts, he was out. The air was cold and clung to his cheeks like melting wax on a candle. As if it were second nature, Walter picked up the gun and turned back toward the window. In order to see into the basement, he had to drop down on his belly. The ground was freezing cold, like sheets of ice. But he put that out of his mind and looked in. Bart wasn't doing very well. The large crab in the doorway was gone and that made for more room at the entrance. Rather than one or two at a time sliding down the staircase, the smaller crabs were now dropping down the staircase five and six at a time.

Walter shouted. "Let's go!"

He aimed and fired. And fired again.

In rapid succession, he squeezed the trigger of his pistol, trying to make each shot count.

Bart turned toward the window and ran, ducking as he did. As much as Walter seemed to make his shots count, he had two facts playing against him. One, there were more crabs ascending the staircase than he had time to aim at. For every one that he took down, two were getting beyond his line of sight. And second, he was blocking part of the open window. And since it was so narrow, Bart needed all the room he could get to climb out. As Deputy Bart Chandler started to climb through the window, his head and right arm extended out into the parking lot, he shouted in pain. He jerked hard, and blood sprayed from his mouth.

"No!" Walter shouted, still firing his gun into the basement.

He squeezed the trigger. One went down. He squeezed the trigger a second and third time. Another went down.

"Help me," Walter shouted.

In his peripheral, he could see Angela trying to help pull the deputy out into the parking lot. The police officer's eyes were wide with pain and shock.

Walter looked into the window right below him. The crabs were clamping onto the officer's legs and stomach.

CLCK...

"Go," Bart gurgled, blood bubbling around the corners of his mouth.

"No," Angela cried, still trying to pull him free.

Determined not to give up, Walter aimed and fired again. This time his weapon *ticked* empty.

"Shit." He tossed the gun down, climbed to his feet and started helping Angela pull Bart through the window.

CLICK... CLICK... CLICK...

Bart groaned and grunted, even more blood spewing from his lips.

And then, he was suddenly free.

Walter and Angela fell back onto their butts onto the cold, hard pavement. When they looked up, Deputy Bart Chandler wasn't moving. He was missing one leg. A blood pool formed around the severed appendage, and a streak of crimson creased the pavement from the open basement window to his current location.

"We have to move," Dotty insisted.

Walter only hesitated long enough to take the deputy's gun. Hopefully it had recently been reloaded.

"We're going to just leave him?" Angela gasped.

"He's dead, Angela." Walter grabbed her by the hand. "And unless we want to end up just like him, we need to move. Dotty's right.... We got to go."

She took a deep breath, which assured him that she was right there with him.

Walter scooped up Lina in one arm and held Angela's hand even tighter with his free hand.

"Now, how do we get out of here?" Walter said, looking to Dotty.

The back parking lot was fenced in and lined with cop cars and golf carts.

Dotty pointed to the gate. "Broomberg never locks it. Used the golf carts on his off days. Just keeps the chain and everything hooked up for show."

Walter, Lina and Angela followed Dotty's lead. She led them to the gate, which had, in fact, only been made to appear locked. She removed the lock and spun the chain out from around the gate, and they were home free.

"Where are we even going?" Angela shouted as Walter pulled her along, leaving the police station's back parking lot behind.

"To the roof," Walter shouted, pulling her along as Dotty led the way around the police station toward the street.

"What roof?" Lina shouted into his ear as she bounced with each giant step he took forward."

"Any roof," he said.

As they rounded the back of the police station toward the street, they realized that they were not alone. The parking lot out in front of the police station was a massive horde of crabs, both giant and small, all seeking entrance into the police station. Since their numbers were so great, they were left wandering the parking lot while there was no room left to fit inside the building.

"I don't think they see us," Angela shouted, Walter tugging her with each frantic step he took forward.

As if her words had been a cue in the movies, all at once the monstrous horde of crabs began to clatter toward them.

CLICK...CLICK...CLICK...

"Just get us to the roof, Dotty." Walter panted as he ran.

Dotty pointed toward a building directly across the adjacent street from the police station. The building she seemed to have in mind was an old style barbershop, with the swirling signage out front.

"There's a ladder to the roof around back," Dotty barked.

"What about the helicopter?" Lina cried.

The things gave chase, steadily closing the gap between them.

CLICK...CLICK...CLICK...

"There it is, right there." Walter pointed as they ran along one side of the barbershop building.

The helicopter appeared in the sky over them, careening toward them from over the top of the police station. With its beaming lights facing down toward them, and the crabs that gave chase, Walter knew that they had been spotted.

"They're getting closer," Angela shouted.

Walter's palm was getting sweaty, but he refused to let go. He squeezed Angela's hand even tighter.

"We're almost there." Dotty rounded the back corner of the barbershop building to reveal an access ladder that went to the roof.

"Thank God," Walter said, forcing Angela in front of the ladder. "Go."

"Lina."

"No, I got her. Go."

As soon as she was up a few rungs, Walter began to climb using only the one hand while still holding Lina tightly against his chest.

Then several military style helicopters blew past from overhead, aiming down toward the horde that were perusing Walter, Dotty, Angela and Lina. As if the *whooping* thrum of their propellers weren't loud enough, a barrage of machine gun fire belched from above in rapid succession. The horde that was almost on top of Dotty and Walter exploded into bits, chunks of meat and outer bone jutting out and flying in all directions with each passing bullet that rained down.

Dotty and Walter found themselves frozen in place as they watched everything unfold before them. The two additional helicopters readjusted as half a dozen roped men dropped down. Men with M16s on their backs slid down the ropes with rapid ease before dropping to the ground amidst the fallen crabs of mutilated meat. As if trained to perfection, the men had their weapons drawn and aimed toward another oncoming horde as the new wave of creatures grew impatient.

CLICK... CLICK... CLICK...

A hail of fire rained as the streets echoed with gunfire. All six men were aimed and firing into the ascending mob of creatures. Both big and small, the crabs fell, but more took their places.

"There's too many," one soldier shouted between gunfire.

"They're flanking us," another shouted. "Two o'clock. Two o'clock!"

But it was too late.

A giant crab fell on top of one of the soldiers, its massive pincers sheering the man in half with one single clip. The other five men turned, aiming their M16s toward the giant thing. They tore into it with a hail of bullets. The thing jerked as bullets tore it into bits. Blood, meat, and exoskeleton littered the ground around the giant thing as it fell apart with each bullet that passed through it.

Then, even over the noise of rapid fire, someone in one of the helicopters overhead shouted something through an amplified speaker. Whatever had been said, Walter couldn't make out. But whatever it had been it drew all five soldiers' attention away from the thing they had been shooting and toward town.

As they looked, so did Walter and Dotty.

The giant crab to beat all giant crabs was headed right for them. Behind it was another swarm of crabs both big and small. But this one...the one in the lead, it was three times the size of any of the giants Walter had seen so far. It had to be the size of a house. It was easily one story tall and as wide as a three-bedroom, two-bath house with a side garage. It lumbered forward, its generous pincers slamming opened and closed as it drew near.

CLICK... CLICK... CLICK...

The sound of its pincers slamming shut echoed off of the buildings, covering even the sound of the helicopters above.

All five soldiers, not at all concerned about the horde of crabs that followed behind, fired on this one monster crab. Bits of meat and red bone tore away as their bullets penetrated it, but it wasn't stopping. It just kept on coming and didn't slow down.

One of the soldiers pulled something from his waist and tossed it across the parking lot into the street right in front of the thing.

Before the thought *grenade* could enter into Walter's mind, an explosion of dirt, gravel and crabs engulfed the street. For a moment, there was nothing to see as the dirt and dust started to settle. But before it could, the giant, monstrously huge crab darted through the debris and toward the unsuspecting soldiers. It grabbed two of the men, one with each pincer. It snapped one in half, letting both parts of the man fall to the ground, while it shoved the other soldier into its mandibles, biting off his head. The grenade had done nothing to the monster.

The last two standing soldiers fired.

Their weapons were useless. The thing was angry now. It dropped the headless soldier down and charged. One of the soldiers turned to run, but it was too late. The crab reached out, taking him in its grasp. And with one simple squeeze, the soldier fell away in two bloody separate halves.

As the last soldier was being run down, Walter realized the street was starting to becoming overrun once more. If they were going to make it to the roof, they needed to move.

"Come on, Dotty," Walter shouted, but without looking down. He kept on climbing.

Once he was about halfway up the ladder, Angela screamed from above him. "Dotty!"

Walter risked a glance and saw the carnage as it unfolded. Tons of small crabs were trying to get to Dotty, but she was too high up the ladder. That wasn't true, however, for the giant ones.

Three giant crabs rushed to the climbing old woman as one until they simultaneously pulled her down. Dotty's eyes were filled with shock as she locked gazes with Walter right before getting pulled from the ladder. Before her body could hit the cold snow-covered ground, it split into fifteen different pieces. Her blood sprayed down in a crimson show, the crabs lapping it all up with reckless abandon.

Lina started to cry.

With that cue, Walter turned his eyes away from the carnage and started climbing again. When he got to the top, Angela was there accepting her child with grief-stricken terror.

Once Walter was on the roof, he looked back down the ladder toward the creatures feasting on Dotty's scattered viscera. He looked out at the lot, the streets beyond that, and saw that they were filled with those giant and small ocean monsters. The two military copters were firing down on the super crab. Its body twisted and jerked as it fell apart from the ravenous machine gun fire from above. The lone soldier was nowhere to be seen. How he'd managed to make it onto the roof was an utter miracle.

A light shined onto his face as the *whooping* sound got louder and louder. The wind kicked up hard all around them as the helicopter began its descent onto the barbershop rooftop.

Once it landed, Walter Maninko helped Angela climb in before passing Lina up.

Walter and Angela locked gazes as he got onboard. She was covered in blood.

And still just as beautiful as the day they had met all those many years ago.

Epilogue

Walter Maninko's heart filled with joy as the subtle *BEEP...BEEP...BEEP...* of the cash register scanned each item.

One item, one scan, he thought, relishing in the store motto with a smile.

BEEP...BEEP... BEEP....

The Dollar General Store was an utter wreck. As he scanned a few more items, placing them into the bright yellow bags before ringing up the total for the customer, Walter took it all in.

The seasonal section was a disaster. Charcoal bags were all in the wrong places, causing customers to complain when he rang up the item, clearly not giving them the big bag of grilling supplies for the meager dollar that it was listed as. The lanterns were scatted across the aisle floor rather than stationed in their slots on the end-cap display. The bug spray section was completely empty. With plenty of the product in the back room ready to be restocked, there was no telling how long it would be before he managed to get them out onto the sales floor. Or how many people would come in and leave frustrated that the one summer item they came in to get was sold out.

Walter Maninko didn't care. With a genuine smile on his face, he greeted each customer with the enthusiasm of a saint.

He also didn't care that there was a full, unstocked pallet of merchandise currently sitting on the ends of almost every aisle not getting put onto the shelves by his other sales associates. The laundry aisle had a pallet of boxes on either end, literally forming a blockade which forced the customers to turn around, aggravated, as they tried to make their way through the maze of pallets, trash and scattered merchandise that littered the floors.

Walter had two other associates working this shift with him. Neither of them was in sight. They were either outside taking their usual fifteen-minute smoke break, which seemed to happen every hour on the hour, or they were in the back room drinking and eating stolen merchandise rather than running one of the registers or putting out freight.

Walter also observed the long line of disgruntled customers with a heartwarming smile. Some of the faces were new. Others were not. The regulars were easy to spot because they came in every day. Sometimes four and five times a day at that. There was the extreme couponer who made checking out a single customer take seven times as long, her three shopping carts full of Downy Softener. Then there was the guy that drove the thirty-five-thousand-dollar car wearing the three-hundred-dollar sunglasses. Almost every day like clockwork, this shopper loved to come in and buy a dozen Monster energy drinks. But not without paying with his Food Stamp card, of course. It was also hard to forget the meth cooker's face. At least that was what Walter assumed the dingy little man was up to. He came in every day like clockwork, purchasing a single box of pseudoephedrine. His face twitched, and he clearly needed to brush his tooth. It was the only one he had left, and it was looking pretty ripe. With one hand constantly scratching at the sores on his right cheek, Walter couldn't help but wonder if the man needed a Benadryl or a nap. He just looked so miserable.

Walter Maninko took a deep breath of relief, even though his customer line at the register was six people deep. Because honestly, being miserable was the farthest thing from his mind.

The Dollar General might have been a total disaster, but it was his disaster. And no one was going to take that away from him.

Just like no one was going to take away his new life.

Things were great.

He was great.

Angela was great.

Lina was great.

They were his everything. And besides, Angela Maninko had a nice ring to it.

Shortly after that horrific night in Seward, Alaska, Walter and his new family were brought back to Redding, California, free of charge. Although he didn't understand the full scope of the situation, Walter knew that what had happened was essentially a cover-up. There had only been a few survivors of that night, mostly because they had managed to lay low and stay quiet. Of the people who survived, the state bought out any property they might have owned and sent them packing, either to another town within the county, or to any state of their choosing.

Walter's choice of going back to Redding, California, had been a given. But when Angela had decided that she would go with him, it meant the world. Shortly after, the two got married, combining the money they received from the cover-up settlement. This money was used to buy them a nice four-bedroom, two-bath house right near the lake. It was a peaceful spot paid in full.

Angela spent most of her days tending to her garden and reading books. She was still getting used to the idea of summer year 'round.

Although Lina wasn't a Maninko, having kept her biological father's last name, she truly was his daughter. Every moment he got to spend with her was a blessing. A blessing that brightened up even his dreariest of days. Days that, in fact, he hardly ever had anymore.

Things were looking good.

His daughter was coming up on her tenth birthday now, and he and Angela were expecting.

A boy.

Walter even got back into writing. He'd given up on screenplays, however, and surprisingly managed to lock a publishing deal for a three book series called *That Fatal Night*. The series was about a discount store manager who accidently got a glowing orb in with his truck of freight for the store. And when one of his bumbling idiot employees accidently dropped the glowing orb, it shattered, causing a vortex of light that engulfed the store and everyone in it, sending them into a world of dinosaurs, aliens, and robots. He was having a lot of fun writing it and was even using some of his actual employees as characters in the book. He found it so much easier to just write what he knew than to try writing what he thought others might like.

Every day at work was a new adventure that he could incorporate into the stories he worked on at home, after tucking his daughter in for the night.

Life was peaceful and things were finally going his way.

He may still be that lowly old Dollar General Store Manager, but at least he was happy. Every now and again, one of his old friends who were still trying their luck as screenwriters would come in and see him. They felt sorry for him. In their eyes, he was all washed-up. He'd given up on his dream and just settled for a junky little job making nearly minimum wage. In their eyes, he was a loser.

But they couldn't be further from the truth.

Even as they tried telling Walter all about their successes, he couldn't help but smile.

They hadn't been the ones who rushed into town, dragged the love of his life across a snow-covered landscape of horror, saved the day, and won the hearts of the only two people in this world that mattered. No, they didn't do that at all.

That's because they weren't *Walter Maninko*.

"Excuse me, sir." A customer stepped up to the register. "You got any bug spray? The shelf is empty."

"We sure do," Walter said. "Let me go get it for you."

And with that, Walter stepped out from behind the register, leaving the line of people waiting to check out. Each step forward was a chance for him to live his life his way. The right way. The way it had always been meant to be lived.

The Walter Maninko way.

BEEP...BEEP...BEEP...

The End

Afterthoughts by the Author

As the reader, I don't know if you noticed it or not, but this novella was inspired by a series of novels called *CLICKERS*. If you haven't read those books, I highly recommend them. It is a series written by *J. F. Gonzalez* and my favorite horror author, *Brian Keene*. This book is a homage to those two very talented men.

I decided to do an afterward section for this book because I felt it would be appropriate to give a little back story into how this novella actually came about. Why did it even get written?

You see, although I have written more than a dozen horror fiction titles, I don't actually know anything about Alaska, Alaskan king crab, or the crabbing industry. If there is one thing I have always told myself as a writer, it is to write what you know and fill in the rest. So, how is it that I ended up writing a book about creatures and places with which I have no experience? Well, that's easy…and that is what this afterward is here to explain.

In a totally unrelated matter, I recently started designing patches for an online retailer. These patches were doing so well for that store that I got a brilliant idea. Why don't I start designing and selling my own patches? I could make patches about things I like, such as Howard the Duck, old horror movies, UFOs and Bigfoot. It seemed to make sense. So, I did that very thing and looked into what I would need to get the ball rolling for my very own patch store of personal designs. After doing the research, I concluded that I need some money to start my little venture. It was easy enough. Get some money. Start making patches. The end.

Thing is, during the conception of this patch idea, I was a full-time student working for minimum wage with a part-time gig for the *Dollar General*. I didn't have any money to invest.

And then it hit me. I could get an advance if I wrote a book. Seemed easy enough, considering I had gotten advances from a few publishers in the past. So, knowing that *Severed Press* supported me not only as a writer, but as a designer as well, I reached out. And they obliged *(note: Publishers do not just give out advances. I am an established author with a reputation that merits such actions)*. However, it came with a price. I couldn't just write any old thing. It needed to be specific. They were after giant sea creatures to be exact. Also, *That Fatal Night*, the book series that Walter Maninko started writing, was actually one of the pitches I made to the publisher along with this story.

And thus, this novella was born. I managed to write this book while taking 16 credit hours of college and working part-time at the good ol' *Dollar General*.

So, why say all of that?

Well, there are a few morals to this story. One, you are never too busy to write a book. Two, always be thankful for publishers who have your back even when your goal is to start up something unrelated to books. Those blessings are rare and you should be grateful. Three, never just pitch one idea. Not all of them are what the publishers are looking for. And four, always write what you know and fill in the rest.

Thanks for reading this book. If you're interested, you should also check out my patches. Those things are, after all, the entire reason why this book got written in the first place.

Stay Scared,

P. A. Douglas

www.BeardCakes.com

CHECK OUT OTHER GREAT DEEP SEA THRILLERS

MEGATOOTH
by Viktor Zarkov

When the death rate of sperm whales rises dramatically, a well-respected environmental activist puts together a ragtag team to hit the high seas to investigate the matter. They suspect that the deaths are due to poachers and they are all driven by a need for justice.

Elsewhere, an experimental government vessel is enhancing deep sea mining equipment. They see one of these dead whales up close and personal...and are fairly certain that it wasn't poachers that killed it.

Both of these teams are about to discover that poachers are the least of their worries. There is something hunting the whales...

Something big
Something prehistoric.
Something terrifying.
MEGATOOTH!

BLOOD CRUISE
by Jake Bible

Ben Clow's plans are set. Drop off kids, pick up girlfriend, head to the marina, and hop on best friend's cruiser for a weekend of fun at sea. But Ben's happy plans are about to be changed by a tentacled horror that lurks beneath the waves.

International crime lords! Deep cover black ops agents! A ravenous, bloodsucking monster! A storm of evil and danger conspire to turn Ben Clow's vacation from a fun ocean getaway into a nightmare of a Blood Cruise!

CHECK OUT OTHER GREAT DEEP SEA THRILLERS

SEA RAPTOR
by John J. Rust

From terrorist hunter to monster hunter! Jack Rastun was a decorated U.S. Army Ranger, until an unfortunate incident forced him out of the service. He is soon hired by the Foundation for Undocumented Biological Investigation and given a new mission, to search for cryptids, creatures whose existence has not been proven by mainstream science. Teaming up with the daring and beautiful wildlife photographer Karen Thatcher, they must stop a sea monster's deadly rampage along the Jersey Shore. But that's not the only danger Rastun faces. A group of murderous animal smugglers also want the creature. Rastun must utilize every skill learned from years of fighting, otherwise, his first mission for the FUBI might very well be his last.

OCEAN'S HAMMER
by D.J. Goodman

Something strange is happening in the Sea of Cortez. Whales are beaching for no apparent reason and the local hammerhead shark population, previously believed to be fished to extinction, has suddenly reappeared. Marine biologists Maria Quintero and Kevin Hoyt have come to investigate with a television producer in tow, hoping to get footage that will land them a reality TV show. The plan is to have a stand-off against a notorious illegal shark-fishing captain and then go home.

Things are not going according to plan.

There is something new in the waters of the Sea of Cortez. Something smart. Something huge. Something that has its own plans for Quintero and Hoyt.

CHECK OUT OTHER GREAT DEEP SEA THRILLERS

MEGA
by Jake Bible

There is something in the deep. Something large. Something hungry. Something prehistoric.
And Team Grendel must find it, fight it, and kill it.
Kinsey Thorne, the first female US Navy SEAL candidate has hit rock bottom. Having washed out of the Navy, she turned to every drink and drug she could get her hands on. Until her father and cousins, all ex-Navy SEALS themselves, offer her a way back into the life: as part of a private, elite combat Team being put together to find and hunt down an impossible monster in the Indian Ocean. Kinsey has a second chance, but can she live through it?

THE BLACK
by Paul E Cooley

Under 30,000 feet of water, the exploration rig Leaguer has discovered an oil field larger than Saudi Arabia, with oil so sweet and pure, nations would go to war for the rights to it. But as the team starts drilling exploration well after exploration well in their race to claim the sweet crude, a deep rumbling beneath the ocean floor shakes them all to their core. Something has been living in the oil and it's about to give birth to the greatest threat humanity has ever seen.

"The Black" is a techno/horror-thriller that puts the horror and action of movies such as Leviathan and The Thing right into readers' hands. Ocean exploration will never be the same."